Hauptmann

by John Logan

A SAMUEL FRENCH ACTING EDITION

SAMUEL FRENCH

FOUNDED 1830

New York Hollywood London Toronto

SAMUELFRENCH.COM

ISBN   978-0-573-62748-4   Printed   in   U.S.A.   #10574

IMPORTANT BILLING AND CREDIT REQUIREMENTS

All producers of HAUPTMANN *must* give credit to the Author of the Play in all programs distributed in connection with performances of the Play and in all instances in which the title of the Play appears for purposes of advertising, publicizing or otherwise exploiting the Play and/or a production. The name of the Author *must* also appear on a separate line, on which no other name appears, immediately following the title, and *must* appear in size of type not less than fifty percent the size of the title type.

In addition the following credits shall also appear in programs distribution in connection with performances of the Play, and in advertising and publicity for the Play:

World Premier at Stormfield Theatre, Chicago
Terry McCabe Artistic Director

Original Off-Broadway production at the
Cherry Lane Theatre, New York
by Victory Gardens Theatre Company
Dennis Zacek, Artistic Director

World Premier at Stormfield Theatre, Chicago
Terry McCabe Artistic Director

Original Off-Broadway production at the
Cherry Lane Theatre, New York
by Victory Gardens Theatre Company
Dennis Zacek, Artistic Director

THE SETTING

April 3, 1936.

Richard Hauptmann's prison cell on Death Row.

Hauptmann tells his story, and lives it in the retelling. His prison guards play all the other roles. The guards never leave the stage.

The stage is open to allow for swift movement into the central playing area. Upstage center is a small platform that represents Hauptmann's cell. Behind the cell are plain wooden chairs for the guards. The guards always remain dressed in simple, gray prison uniforms.

CHARACTERS

Richard Hauptmann

Six Guards:
> Guard 1 / Charles Lindbergh, Policeman 4
> Guard 2 / Anne Morrow Lindbergh, Landlady
> Guard 3 / Anna Hauptmann, Policeman 5, Reporter 2, Edna Ferber
> Guard 4 / Prosecuting Attorney Wilentz, Policeman 2, Reporter 1, Eddie Mahar, Priest 1
> Guard 5 / Dr. Condon, Policeman 1, Reporter 3, Bailiff, Arthur Koehler (wood expert), Albert Osborne (handwriting expert), Amandus Hochmuth (elderly witness), Hawker, Alexander Woolcott, H.L. Mencken
> Guard 6 / Judge Trenchard, Policeman 3, Reporter 4, Damon Runyon, Priest 2

AUTHOR'S NOTE

It is not the purpose of this play to present a point by point refutation of the prosecution's case against Richard Hauptmann, those who are interested in this aspect of the story are encouraged to read several recent books which re-examine the case: SCAPEGOAT by Anthony Scaduto, THE AIRMAN AND THE CARPENTER by Ludovic Kennedy and THE LINDBERGH CASE by Jim Fisher.

All I have is a voice
To undo the folded lie,
The romantic lie in the brain
Of the sensual man-in-the-street
And the lie of Authority
Whose buildings grope the sky:
There is no such thing as the State
And no-one exists alone;
Hunger allows no choice
To the citizen or the police;
We must love one another or die.

W.H. Auden

For David Downs

"To be a poet, most of all, to see."

Ibsen

ACT I

(Darkness.)

JUDGE TRENCHARD. Bruno Richard Hauptmann, you have been found guilty of the murder of Charles Lindbergh Jr. There has been no recommendation for life imprisonment. The sentence of this court is that you suffer death at a time and place and in the manner provided by law.

(The lights slowly come up to reveal RICHARD HAUPTMANN sitting in his jail cell. The guards are gathered around the outside of the cell, standing and leaning casually against the bars as they watch him. HAUPTMANN speaks directly to the AUDIENCE in a German accent.)

HAUPTMANN. My name is Bruno Richard Hauptmann. Well, call me Richard anyway. I never really liked the Bruno. It always seemed to me to be a little bit unsavory. In America anything Teutonic is seen as slightly unsavory. In Germany I don't mind being called Bruno so much.

You can also call me "Lone-Wolf Hauptmann" or "Baby-Killer Hauptmann" or "Bloodthirsty Bruno" or "Hauptmann the Damned." I have even heard "Mad-Dog Hauptmann." *(Pause.)*

You can also call me Number 17400. That is what they call me. *(He gestures without looking toward the guards.)*

Are they still looking at me? I know that they are. Sooner or later, I think, I must see every guard, worker, and member of prison staff, as well as their relatives, friends, barbers, newsboys, tailors and pets.

It seems to me that since I was arrested some time ago I have been as a man on a life raft — all surrounded by a sea of eyes. But soon that will end. They tell me that before I am electrocuted a black leather mask is drawn over my face. This is to hide the inevitable contortions from the witnesses. But to me it will be a curtain to separate me from the eyes.

You notice the light? It is never off. That is so the eyes can always watch. They think I will do myself some harm. Hang myself with a blanket or slowly cut through my wrists with the edge of my cot. They took away my belt and my shoe laces for that reason. I find it comforting to know I will go to my death in slippers. *(Pause.)*

I am also shaved. A nice young man named Joe comes in every day and shaves my face. We talk for a little bit every morning and he tells me about the day outside, about the weather and such. I tell him about the light and the eyes. He is nice to me and talks openly. But he will not look me in the eye.

It is good to talk. *(Pause.)*

They wake me up at six o'clock every morning so I can sit here on my cot. I read the Bible when I can stand to. When there are not too many guards watching I go to the bathroom.

I can always tell when they are bringing food because I can hear the cell block door being opened a long way away. It clangs once loudly and then echoes three times clearly. Although it is a big cell block I am the only guest. I don't see how they can stay in business this way.

No, actually I do have one companion in this block. A few feet away, through thick inches of metal, is the chair. My chair. At first I thought it was morbid to keep me so close to it. But then I decided they were only trying to be efficient. You know the American passion for efficiency. Not so efficient that they could save electricity by turning off the damn light or put some other people in the cell block, but efficient enough to make my last walk a short one. Short in length, I say, but long in depth.

I see my lawyers every day. We talk about appeals and mistrials and stays and commutations.

Sometimes they let me see my wife. *(Pause.)*

When it comes down to it I suppose I should consider myself lucky that I have the knowledge of my end so long before it happens.

Few men have the opportunity to prepare themselves in such detail. I am able to leave no thread hanging — everything is "peachy."

At times I have been fervently religious. I prayed to the Good Lord above to pity and spare an innocent man. It came as a great shock to realize that the Good Lord above is not more merciful than the State of New Jersey.

But still I try to pray. I must be very quiet so they don't come and watch me. But I try anyway.

Forgive me for going on so, but I know the moments are brief that we can share, so I long to say everything before it is too late. I want to record everything that is happening and everything that has happened as if onto stone. Because once it is said it can never be drawn back. I speak and it is forever. Or at least as far as forever goes. Maybe only until the breath is out of the words, maybe until I am killed. Maybe years after that.

I will tell you my story. So you can see it from my eyes and — perhaps — understand. I hope that some part of you will hear and some part of you will believe and question them who did this. Not to vindicate Richard Hauptmann, *but to see that this can never happen again. (Pause. He smiles.)*

I became the baby-killer one year, six months and fifteen days ago.

(He steps from his cell area to the larger playing area downstage. As he speaks lights come up around the stage.)

Wednesday, September 19th, 1900 and 34.

It seemed to me to be an ordinary day. I got up like every morning and my wife, Anna, made breakfast. We talked for a little while about this and that until it was time for me to leave for work. I was going to Manhattan, Wall Street, to work on the stocks.

I suppose it was about seven o' clock when I kissed Manfred, my son, goodbye and went out the front door. I think I remember it was a cool morning, but sunny too. Frost covered the lawn and glimmered on the baby carriage. I unlocked the garage and got into my car. I started the car, backed out of the garage and started driving to work. I drove careful, like I did always. When I think back it amazes me.

These were the last few moments of my life. I mean *my* — Richard Hauptmann's — life. Soon my life would be so altered and changed and perverted that I cannot now recognize myself as the same man who kissed his son, went out of his front door, unlocked his garage and started driving to work.

That man is someone else. Someone much less important and exciting than I am.

So, I was driving to work and suddenly I noticed a big truck, moving truck I think, pull out and block my way. I put pressure on the brake and slow my car to a stop. I glance toward the driver of the truck. I lean back in my seat ... I fold my arms ... and my life is changed.

(Four of the GUARDS, as POLICE OFFICERS, rush forward, grab HAUPTMANN and begin to frisk him.)

HAUPTMANN *(To POLICE:)* Was ist los —? [What is this —?]
POLICEMAN 1. Shut up.
POLICEMAN 2. Are you Bruno Richard Hauptmann?
HAUPTMANN. Wha—?
POLICEMAN 2. Are you Bruno Richard Hauptmann?
HAUPTMANN. I don't see--
POLICEMAN 3. Shut up and answer him.
POLICEMAN 2. Are you Bruno Richard Hauptmann?
HAUPTMANN. Yes, yes. *(The POLICEMEN glance at each other.)* Please, what is th—?
POLICEMAN 1. Is this your car? *(HAUPTMANN does not respond.)* Is this your car?
HAUPTMANN. Ya.
POLICEMAN 3. License number 4U-13-41?
HAUPTMANN. I don't —
POLICEMAN 3. License number 4U-13-41?
HAUPTMANN. I'm not sure. I think so, ya.

(The POLICEMEN drag HAUPTMANN upstage into the cell area which now represents the bedroom in the Hauptmann home. They throw him on the cell cot.)

HAUPTMANN. They made me drive my car back home and brought me upstairs to my bedroom where they continued questioning me.

(Two of the POLICEMEN begin to tear apart the bedroom/cell. In mime they tear off wall boards, open books, flip through them and toss them to the floor. They casually toss aside personal items.)

POLICEMAN 4. Do you own a Stanley three-quarter inch chisel?

HAUPTMANN. Yes.

POLICEMAN 4. Where is your tool box?

HAUPTMANN. In the garage.

POLICEMAN 4. Do you own a planer?

HAUPTMANN. Yes. *(He speaks to the POLICEMEN tearing apart the room.)* Please be careful with th—-

POLICEMAN 1. Shut up. Do you frequent the Warner-Quinlan gas station?

HAUPTMANN. The what?

POLICEMAN 4. The Warner-Quinlan gas station.

HAUPTMANN. Which one?

POLICEMAN 4. The Bronx.

HAUPTMANN. I must, yes.

POLICEMAN 1. Have you ever been to Horseneck Beach near Elizabeth Island?

HAUPTMANN. *(To AUDIENCE:)* All this time I am wondering, where is Anna? Have they got her too? Why are they—?

POLICEMAN 1. Have you ever been at Horseneck Beach near Elizabeth Island?

HAUPTMANN. No.

POLICEMAN 1. Do you recognize this telephone number: DG 3-7154?

HAUPTMANN. I'm not sure.

POLICEMAN 1. DG 3-7154?

HAUPTMANN. No.

POLICEMAN 3. Have you ever been in Woodlawn cemetery?

HAUPTMANN. No.

POLICEMAN 1. Have you ever been in New Jersey?

HAUPTMANN. Sure.

POLICEMAN 1. When?

HAUPTMANN. On carpentry jobs. I don't remember when.

POLICEMAN 1. When was the last time?

HAUPTMANN. *(To AUDIENCE:)* All the while they were questioning me they were tearing apart my house. I watched while they stripped off the wallpaper and the boards. They flipped through all the books and dumped them onto the floor. They knocked all of our pictures out of the way —

POLICEMAN 2. When was the last time you were in New Jersey?

HAUPTMANN. I'm not sure. Three or four months ago.

POLICEMAN 2. What about in 1932?

HAUPTMANN. 1932?

POLICEMAN 2. Yeah.

HAUPTMANN. More then.

POLICEMAN 1. Why?

HAUPTMANN. Because 1 worked more as a carpenter then. I work now more on Manhattan, Wall Street —

(One of the POLICEMEN holds up a bill in front of HAUPTMANN.)

POLICEMAN 3. Did you pass this bill at the Warner-Quinlan gas station in the Bronx?

HAUPTMANN. I don't know.

POLICEMAN 3. It's a gold certificate bill, look closely.

(ANNA HAUPTMANN enters escorted by police. She is distraught.)

HAUPTMANN. Anna —

POLICEMAN 3. Do you remember this bill?

HAUPTMANN. No.

ANNA. Was ist los, Richard? [What is this, Richard?]

HAUPTMANN. Ich weiss nicht. Ich verstehe nicht was — [I don't know. I don't understand what —]

(He stands to go to her and is pushed back onto the cot.)

ANNA. Richard —

POLICEMAN 1. Have you ever been to St. Raymond's cemetery?

HAUPTMANN. Keine sorge, Anna. [Don't worry, Anna.]

POLICEMAN 1. Have you ever been to St. Raymond's cemetery?

HAUPTMANN. I don't know.

ANNA. Warum tun es sie? Ich verstehe nicht. [Why are they doing this? I don't understand.]

HAUPTMANN. Anna, ruhe. Sag nichts. [Anna, be quiet. Don't say anything.]

POLICEMAN 2. Hey, in English.

HAUPTMANN. I told my wife she should not to worry.

POLICEMAN 3. How do you get to New Jersey when you go?

HAUPTMANN. One of the bridges.

POLICEMAN 3. Which one?

HAUPTMANN. I don't know. *(The POLICEMEN chat among themselves.)* Anna, where's Manfred?

ANNA. I was out in the backyard. Manfred was playing next to me on the grass. I didn't hear you come back in. I saw a shadow over me and I thought it was you, I thought you had come back. It was a policeman. He told me to come inside for questioning. Richard, I don't know what is happening —

HAUPTMANN. Shhh, keine sorge, Anna. [Don't worry, Anna.]

ANNA. I left Manfred with Emily next door.

HAUPTMANN. Good.

ANNA. Have you done something wrong, Richard?

POLICEMAN 2. How do you spell the word "boat"?

(Beat.)

HAUPTMANN. What?

POLICEMAN 2. How do you spell the word "boat"?

HAUPTMANN: B-O-

ANNA. Richard —?

HAUPTMANN. -A-T.

POLICEMAN 1. Have you ever met Dr. John F. Condon?

HAUPTMANN. No.

POLICEMAN 1. What newspaper do you read?

HAUPTMANN. The *Bronx Home News. (The POLICEMEN glance at each other.)* Please, tell me what —

POLICEMAN 2. Have you ever met Dr. John F. Condon?

HAUPTMANN. I told you, no.

ANNA. *(Realizing:)* Mein Gott —

POLICEMAN 2: Have you ever been in Hopewell, New Jersey?

HAUPTMANN. No.

ANNA. Mein Gott —!

POLICEMAN 2. Have you ever met Colonel Charles Lindbergh?

HAUPTMANN. What?

POLICEMAN 2. Have you ever met Colonel Charles Lindbergh?

(Pause.)

HAUPTMANN. What do you say?

POLICEMAN 2. Have you ever met Colonel Charles Lindbergh?

HAUPTMANN. *No.*

ANNA. Richard —

(HAUPTMANN lurches forward into the downstage area.)

HAUPTMANN. St. Raymond's cemetery ... The gold certificate bill ... Dr. Condon ... Hopewell, New Jersey! Of course! It was all clear. They wanted me for the Lindbergh kidnapping! They thought I had killed the little Lindbergh baby. They thought I had something to do with it, or knew somebody or was somehow connected. *(Pause.)*

At first I could not believe. I raced with my mind back to see what could have happened. Where did I fit into a crime that happened two years earlier? Poor Anna was terrified. I told her not to worry. I told her ... *everything would be fine ... (Pause.)*

Colonel Charles Lindbergh.

(The guard playing Lindbergh steps into the light. His familiar blond hair shines with an angelic glow.)

He was God. Or so you would think to hear some people talk.

Some people?! The whole of America revered Charles Lindbergh. Why? *(He shrugs.)*

At eight o' clock on the morning of May 20th in 1927 he got into a little plane and flew to Europe in 33 hours. He did this alone. "The Lone Eagle" they called him. He was a hero. When he arrived in New York bushel upon bushel of little scraps of paper were showered on his head.

(ANNE MORROW LINDBERGH joins her husband. They wave as reporters flash pictures. They freeze in this tableau. There is a pause as HAUPTMANN, bemused, watches them for a moment.)

The Lindberghs. They had anything that was of value in this country. They had wealth, social position, grace, and that certain removed superiority that America demands from her idols. They stood above and beyond the concerns and problems of you and me. They stood: the Ideal of American Success. *(Pause. Then softly:)*

It seemed they *glimmered*. Glimmering, they passed through their charmed lives. Every step was right, every gesture, intonation, glance and thought was ideal. Glimmering and ideal.

Now when I think back it amazes me that my life could have become so involved with that famous couple. Anna and I were so limited. Always counting pennies, saving receipts and looking through the paper for whatever sales there might be. Anna and I had to watch our money. It is a hard life for two immigrants. And when I look at photographs of Mrs. Lindbergh I wish I too could buy my wife nice dresses, and give her jewels to wear around the neck. I wanted to fly with my wife too. *(Pause. He smiles with remembrance.)*

I remember one night, though. This was a few years ago. It was Anna's birthday and I decided to spend a little of our money to go out special. There was one thing my wife had often talked about doing. One little treat she wanted. She wanted to go into New York City and see the motion picture. So I thought, okay, a special birthday. We had dinner and dressed in our church clothes. We drove special into the city — and paid for parking — and went to the movie theatre. The name of the picture I still remember. It was called "Top Hat" and it starred Mr. Astaire and Mrs. Rogers. Oh, and it was so beautiful.

(As he speaks Irving Berlin's "Cheek to Cheek" begins to play and the LINDBERGHS begin a beautiful and intricate Astaire-Rogers dance. With cold, emotionless faces they spin and swirl around the stage as HAUPTMANN speaks.)

They wore lovely clothes and spoke such good English! The story was very complicated and I can't really sort through it all, but it ended well for them all. She was very pretty and American and he was very funny and clever. Never insulting, you understand, but smart. He wanted to make love to her so they danced together several times. My wife liked best the dancing, of course. They danced so nicely. And Anna I and were so happy —

(Suddenly REPORTERS break into the Lindberghs' dance and begin snapping photographs and shouting questions.)

REPORTER 1. Colonel Lindbergh! Do you have any idea who would want to —?
REPORTER 2. Mrs. Lindbergh do you plan to have anymore children?
REPORTER 3. Do you have any idea who would want to kidnap your baby?!
REPORTER 4. Do you think it was organized crime?
REPORTER 2. Do you think it was an inside job?
REPORTER 4. How much will you pay for your baby?
REPORTER 3. Colonel Lindbergh, do you think the child is alive?
REPORTER 1. Do you think the baby is dead?

(ANNE LINDBERGH fades into darkness as CHARLES LINDBERGH steps forward to make a statement. He raises his hand for silence.)

LINDBERGH. My wife and I would like to make a statement: Mrs. Lindbergh and I wish to make personal contact with the kidnappers of our child — *(The REPORTERS flare up with questions. When they are silent LINDBERGH continues.)* Our only interest is in the safe return of our child —

HAUPTMANN. The ransom note read: "Dear Sir. Have $50,000 redy. $25,000 in $20 bills; $15,000 in $10 bills and $10,000 in $5 bills —

LINDBERGH. We urge those who have the child to select any representative who will be suitable to them at any time and any place they may designate —

HAUPTMANN. "After 2 or 4 days we will tell wer to deliver the mony. We warn you not to mak anycling public or for notifying the police —

LINDBERGH. We have all confidence that our son is safe and we hope to cooperate with whatever demands the kidnappers make —

HAUPTMANN. "The child is in gut care. And all notes will haf dis singnature with three holes."

LINDBERGH. Thank you.

(The REPORTERS shout questions and follow LINDBERGH to the rear of the stage. HAUPTMANN is alone.)

HAUPTMANN. Like millions of other people on Wednesday morning the 2nd of March in 1932 I opened my newspaper to see that Charles Lindbergh Junior had been taken from his crib the night before. Someone had broken into the secluded house and kidnapped the child.

Hopewell, New Jersey became the center of the world. The house was beset by reporters who arrived in great packs and scoured the grounds for any missed clues, for any "hot leads." Anything that could bring the kidnappers to quick justice.

Oh, please note I say "kidnappers." Everyone was convinced it was the act of a gang. No one would believe it was the product of a single mind. Only after my arrest did everyone claim that, yes, it certainly was the job of a lone-wolf and they had really thought so all along.

To kidnap the golden haired baby of such a great hero? Who could do such a thing? What kind of monster was this? These ques-

tions I asked myself that morning. Like everyone else I wanted hard justice for the kidnappers. *(He smiles.)*
Considering the outcome I might have been less pugnacious.
For weeks the shadowy figure of the kidnapper *haunted* America. He was seen in every playground and at every school. Mothers thought they saw him in postmen, bus drivers, delivery boys, school-teachers ...
And still, through all this, there was no real word from the kidnappers. It was an unearthly quiet more terrifying than the outrage following the crime. It was the silence of death. Like those swift, eternal seconds after a bomb has stopped ticking. Every nerve is tensed for the explosion ... *(Pause.)*
Finally, Mrs. Lindbergh made an announcement over the radio.

(A pale ANNE LINDBERGH steps into the light and speaks.)

ANNE LINDBERGH. An open appeal to whomever has my child. Please adhere to the following diet: a half cup of orange juice on waking; one quart of milk during the day; two teaspoons of cooked vegetables once a day; one baked potato or rice once a day — *(She falters.)* Three tablespoons of cooked cereal morning and night.

(She steps into the darkness.)

HAUPTMANN. Hundreds of false leads were researched and thousands of letters came to the Hopewell house demanding money for the safe return of the child. But all these letters lacked that special signature: a symbol made up of two interlocking circles and three square holes.
The police were very active. They were convinced it was an "inside job." You see the Lindberghs only spent weekends at the Hopewell house — from Friday to Monday. Yet on that particular weekend they had decided to stay through Tuesday because the baby had a slight cold and his mother didn't want to move him. The baby was taken on that Tuesday night. *(Pause.)*
Who could have known the Lindberghs were going to stay an extra day? Who could have known the schedule they had followed for

months would be broken on that particular Tuesday? Only the inside staff of the house and whomever they might have contacted. Who else would know this? Would Richard Hauptmann know this? Anyone not connected with the people in the house? No!

I say no.

The police finally centered their questioning on a sprightly English housemaid named Violet Sharpe. She had telephoned her boyfriend the night of the kidnapping to tell him that they were planning to stay at the Hopewell house. Miss Sharpe also had trouble explaining her actions on the day of the crime. She had gone out with a man:

Who was this man? She didn't remember his name.

What did he look like? Oh, average.

What was he wearing? She couldn't remember.

Were you alone? No, with two other people.

Who were they? She couldn't remember.

What had they done? Gone to a movie.

What movie? She couldn't remember.

Where was the movie? She couldn't remember.

Who appeared in the movie? She couldn't remember!

What was it about? She couldn't remember!

Violet Sharpe had no answers and the police were convinced they had broken the case. They questioned her for hours and when they returned the next day to question her again — *(Pause.)*

When they returned the next day to question her again, Violet Sharpe swallowed a box of rat poison and died. Violet Sharpe was dead and for the police that lead was also dead. Never to be pursued.

And during all this drama no one paid much attention to the busy activity of an old man in the Bronx.

(DR. CONDON steps into the light.)

Dr. John F. Condon. Seventy-two years old. A former educator and insistent pedagogue. Dr. Condon, a severely patriotic American and devoted fan of Charles Lindbergh, decided the waiting had gone on long enough and he was going to do something about it. So he wrote a letter to the editor of the *Bronx Home News.*

CONDON. "I offer all I can possibly do so a loving mother may have her child and Colonel Lindbergh may know that the American people are grateful for the honor bestowed upon them by his pluck and daring.

"I offer myself as a go-between. Let the kidnappers know that no testimony of mine, or information from me, shall be used against them.

"All I ask for myself is the great privilege of putting the baby's arms around his mother's neck once again.

"Sincerely Yours, John F. Condon."

HAUPTMANN. This letter was published in the *Bronx Home News* on March 7th of 1932 and to everyone's great surprise — including, I must admit, Dr. Condon's — he received a letter on March 9th from the kidnappers saying:

"Dearest Sir. If you are prepared to act as go-between in Lindbergh case plese follow strictly instructions. Don't tell anyone about dis. As soon as we find out that the Press or Police is notified everyding are cancel and it will be further delay.

"After you git the mony from Mr. Colonel Lindbergh put these words in the *New York American*: 'The mony is ready.'

"After notice we will give you furder instructions. Be home every night between six to twelve by this time you will hear from us. Do not feel fear — the baby is well." *(Pause.)*

Lindbergh and Dr. Condon met and made plans for gathering the money. They decided the old man needed some kind of code-name to be known by. Dr. Condon, a great lover of anagrams and word games, decided to make a collection of his own initials: J.F.C.

CONDON. Jafsie!

HAUPTMANN. How clever. So on March 10th the following message appeared in the *New York American*:

CONDON: "I accept. The money is ready. Jafsie."

HAUPTMANN. And the waiting began ... *(LINDBERGH and CONDON chat between themselves as they nervously pace the stage.)* Every night the old man and Colonel Lindbergh would pace the aged carpets of Dr. Condon's Bronx home and wait for the ring of the telephone. March 11th:

CONDON. "I accept. The money is ready. Jafsie."

HAUPTMANN. No word. March 12th:

CONDON. "I accept. The money is ready. Jafsie. '

HAUPTMANN. March 12th, 1932. *(CONDON and LIND-BERGH suddenly stop.)* The kidnappers made contact.

CONDON. *(Reading from note:)* "Mr. Condon, we trust you but will not come to your haus it is too danger. Even you cannot know if Police or Secret Service is watching you.

"Follow dis instruction. Take car and drive to last subway station from Jerome Avenue. Here 100 feet from the station to the left, you cross the street and follow the fence along the cemetery. I will meet you there."

HAUPTMANN *(A whisper:)* "I will meet you there ..."

(The stage gradually grows dark.)

It was a cold and very dark night when Dr. Condon drove to the designated meeting spot. It was a lonely place and the sharp wind scattered old newspapers and garbage across the dark street. It appeared to be deserted as Dr. Condon stopped his car and slowly began walking along the iron fence that surrounded Woodlawn cemetery.

(CONDON cautiously walks around the stage as HAUPTMANN speaks.)

All the world had followed this crime to its furthest possibilities, but no one knew that at this moment its climax had been achieved. Here was the first contact with ... the kidnappers!

(HAUPTMANN holds out an overcoat and looks around for someone to play the role of the kidnapper. All the guards turn away and refuse. He scans the audience. Long Pause. He resigns himself to the part and slowly puts on the coat.)

While the good people of the Bronx slept, Dr. Condon was making history.

The old man carefully picked his way over heaps of dead leaves and around benches as he followed the cemetery gate away from the pools of light cast by the street lamps left behind. As his eyes became accustomed to the dark he could see the dim outline of tombstones on the other side of the fence. Now and then the wind would blow a branch across a grave and it would appear to be the shadow of a man. Perhaps a man holding a child?

A sound. Sharp and clear. Close. *(Pause.)*

From the other side of the fence Dr. Condon heard ... breathing.

(Suddenly, from the darkness, a hand reaches out and grabs CON-DON's shoulder. In these scenes HAUPTMANN plays the kid-napper "John" dressed in a heavy overcoat with collar turned up. DR. CONDON cries out as he is grabbed.)

JOHN. Quiet! *(CONDON is still.)* Did you bring the money?

CONDON. I — what I —

JOHN. Did you bring the money?

CONDON. Not until we know we are dealing with the right parties.

JOHN. This is too dangerous —

CONDON. No, please, don't be afraid. I'll be square with you if you'll be square with me.

JOHN. It is too dangerous. It might be twenty years. Or burn. Would I burn if the baby is dead?

CONDON. Dead?! But the baby isn't dead —

JOHN. No, no. The baby isn't dead. It is in good health and getting all that Mrs. Lindbergh asked for. More even. The mother shouldn't worry. Colonel Lindbergh shouldn't worry. You shouldn't worry.

CONDON. How do I know I am talking to the right man?

JOHN. You got the letter with the circular signature and the holes?

CONDON. Yes.

JOHN. Well, then.

CONDON. But, please, what are these.

(He holds up something.)

JOHN. The safety pins. Those are the safety pins that held the baby in the crib. The blanket.

CONDON. Well, I suppose there can be no doubt.

JOHN. There is no doubt.

(Pause.)

CONDON. What's your name?

JOHN. John.

CONDON. What a coincidence. My name is John too. Are you German?

JOHN. No. Scandinavian.

CONDON. What would your mother say, John, if she knew you were mixed up in something like this?

JOHN. She would cry.

CONDON. Then why don't you leave it. I have some money of my own I could give you and —-

JOHN. We don't want your money.

CONDON. We. Who are "we"?

JOHN. The gang. I am only a go-between you see. The head of the gang is Number One, and he is a very big man. He once worked for your government. Number Two is also very smart. He knows you and he told the gang that you are a "good egg."

CONDON. Well then, perhaps Number Two and I could meet. That might facilitate further arrangements.

JOHN. How do you say — "facili--"?

CONDON. Facilitate. It might make things easier if I could talk directly to Number Two.

JOHN. No, that is impossible.

CONDON. Why?

JOHN. Because you would recognize him, of course.

CONDON. Why don't you drop this thing and play it straight! I will give you some money and I'm sure the Lindberghs would help you if you will help us to recover the child.

JOHN. That is impossible.

CONDON. Why?

JOHN. The leader would smack me up. They would drill me.

CONDON. You will be caught.

JOHN. Never.

CONDON. Where is the baby now?

JOHN. He is on a boat. Two women are taking care of him. They take good care of him.

CONDON. How can we recognize the boat?

JOHN. This we will tell you when we have the money.

(Pause.)

CONDON. What will your share of this be?

JOHN. Twenty thousand is to go to Number One. The other five members of the gang get ten thousand each.

CONDON. But that makes seventy thousand! The original sum requested was fifty thousand.

JOHN. Yes, but Mr. Lindbergh has not followed our original instructions. He has called in the police and that makes things a little more difficult. We need to think of ourselves, no? Maybe we will need lawyers? We have to put aside money for lawyers.

CONDON. John, take me to the baby—

(JOHN shakes his head and looks around nervously.)

JOHN. I must be going now, Doctor. You should have brought the money. That would have facil-ita-ted matters.

CONDON. So long as I am satisfied that the baby is well it will be possible to arrange payment. I promised to help Colonel Lindbergh and Mrs. Lindbergh get their baby back. That is all I am out for.

JOHN. Yes, yes, soon you will have the baby. *(He smiles.)* And you can put the baby's arms around his mother's neck.

CONDON. But I must know we are dealing with the right party.

JOHN. We are the right party. On Monday morning we will send you proof.

CONDON. What sort of proof?

(JOHN pats CONDON on the cheek and immediately turns and disappears into darkness. Lights up on HAUPTMANN.)

HAUPTMANN. True to their word, the next week there came in

the mail for Dr. Condon a brown paper package. With some trepidation Dr. Condon carefully tore it open and out fell a little yellow sleeping suit. It fell to his rug and he knelt down to examine it. It was a small pair of Dr. Denton's. And this convinced Colonel Lindbergh. Never mind that this exact suit could have been bought at any of a thousand dime stores, Colonel Lindbergh was convinced.

Along with the suit was a letter with the familiar circular signature and holes. The letter read simply: "Tell mother that baby is well." And that day in the *New York American* appeared:

CONDON. "I accept. Money is ready. Your package is okay. Jafsie."

HAUPTMANN. And so they waited. Dr. Condon waited. Colonel Lindbergh waited. Mrs. Lindbergh waited.

CONDON. "I accept. The money is ready. John, your package is delivered and okay. Please direct me. Jafsie."

HAUPTMANN. And on April 1st, one month to the day after the baby was taken, came more words from the kidnappers. The following night Dr. Condon and Colonel Lindbergh were to drive to a secluded area in the Bronx, again near a cemetery. Only this time they were to carry $70,000 in cash.

(CONDON and LINDBERGH move into action, preparing to meet JOHN. LINDBERGH carries a wooden box about the size of a briefcase.)

They rushed around and gathered the money. A wooden box was constructed to suit the exact specifications of the kidnappers. They drove to a spot near St. Raymond's cemetery and waited. As they stood by the car their breath turned into smoke.

Occasionally they heard a dog barking in a distant alley. The time for the meeting came and went. But still they waited ...

CONDON. Perhaps ---
LINDBERGH. No.
CONDON. They may have been delayed, of course.
LINDBERGH. I'm sure that's it.

(Pause.)

CONDON. How long should we wait?

LINDBERGH. Until they come. *(Pause.)* I can't face my wife until this is done.

CONDON. Of course ...

LINDBERGH. She hasn't slept. Nightmares. *(Pause.)* It's like ... war.

(From the darkness:)

JOHN. Hey, doctor! *(CONDON and LINDBERGH freeze.)* Hey, doctor! Over here! *(LINDBERGH and CONDON exchange a brief glance and then CONDON rushes off into the darkness with the wooden box. LINDBERGH fades into darkness as CONDON meets JOHN inside the cemetery.)* Did you think I wasn't coming?

CONDON. Well, I didn't know.

JOHN. I was watching you two. *(Pause.)* Is that ... ?

CONDON. Colonel Lindbergh.

JOHN. He looks taller in the newsreels.

CONDON. Well, it's dark here.

JOHN. True. *(Pause.)* You brought the money.

CONDON. Yes.

JOHN. Give it to me.

CONDON. Not until I know where the boat with the child is.

(JOHN holds up a piece of paper.)

JOHN. It's all written here, friend. *(CONDON reaches for the note. JOHN withdraws it.)* Do not open the note for six hours, agreed?

CONDON. Agreed.

(They stand looking at each other.)

JOHN. So this is it.
CONDON. This is it.

(At the same moment they exchange the note and the money.)

JOHN. The gang thinks you're fine. Your work has been perfect.

(JOHN turns to leave.)

CONDON. John! *(JOHN stops.)* If we recover the baby and everything is fine, then everything will be fine with you. But if there is anything wrong with this — I swear I will hunt you down. And you will burn.

(JOHN smiles.)

JOHN. Doctor, you will never see me again.

(JOHN disappears into the darkness. Lights come up on LIND-BERGH and ANNE LINDBERGH reading John's note. They are very excited. As they speak, one by one four POLICEMEN form a line upstage of them, watching impassively. HAUPTMANN stands to one side, also watching.)

LINDBERGH. "The boy is on the Boad Nelly —'
ANNE LINDBERGH:. "Boad"?
LINDBERGH. "On the Boad Nelly. It is a small boad 28 feet long —"
ANNE LINDBERGH. "Two persons are on the boad. They are innocent —"
LINDBERGH. "You will find the boad between Horseneck Beach and Gayhead near Elizabeth Island."

(They hug. The POLICEMEN speak immediately, without any emotion:)

POLICEMAN 1, Colonel Lindbergh —
POLICEMAN 2. I hate to be the one to tell —
POLICEMAN 3. Let me give you our utmost sympathy —
POLICEMAN 5. But your baby has been found —
POLICEMAN 2. Dead.
POLICEMAN 1. Discovered in a ditch —

POLICEMAN 2. In a ditch nearby —
POLICEMAN 3. There for weeks —
POLICEMAN 1. Skull crushed —
POLICEMAN 2. Shallow grave —
POLICEMAN 3. Please let me express —
POLICEMAN 5. Sorrow —
POLICEMAN 2. Great regret —
POLICEMAN 1. Tragedy.

(Lights dim on this scene. Lights snap up very sharply on HAUPTMANN being interrogated. He is sitting in a chair with a brutal, strong light over him. He holds a clipboard. Three POLICEMEN stand around him. They have been at it for hours and HAUPTMANN's reserve is cracking.)

POLICEMAN 1. Write.
HAUPTMANN. Not again.
POLICEMAN 1. Write it.

(He writes as they dictate.)

POLICEMAN 3. "Nelly doubted anything —"
POLICEMAN 1. Spell that A-N-Y-D-I-N-G.
POLICEMAN 3. "Would come of investing her money —"
POLICEMAN 1. Spell that M-O-N-Y.
POLICEMAN 3. "In the boat —"
POLICEMAN 1. Spell that B-O-A-D.
POLICEMAN 3. "Factory. Betty had a good —"
POLICEMAN 1. Spell that G-U-T.
POLICEMAN 3. "Number —"
POLICEMAN 1. Spell that N-O-M-E-R.
POLICEMAN 3. "Of people she could ask for money —"
POLICEMAN 1. Spell that —
HAUPTMANN. I know.
POLICEMAN 3. "But she needed a signature —"
POLICEMAN 1. Spell that S-I-*N*-G-N-A-T-U-R-E.
POLICEMAN 3. "To complete her investment."

POLICEMAN 1. And then sign your name. *(They wait for HAUPTMANN to finish.)* Good. Again.

HAUPTMANN. No.

POLICEMAN 1. Again.

HAUPTMANN. Not again, please ...

(POLICEMAN 3 slaps HAUPTMANN.)

POLICEMAN 1. Again, please.

(POLICEMAN 2 intervenes. Takes the clip board from HAUPTMANN.)

POLICEMAN 2. Bruno, you're getting pretty tired of all this aren't you?

HAUPTMANN. I have been here all night —

POLICEMAN 2. Pretty tired, huh?

HAUPTMANN. Ya.

POLICEMAN 2. You'd like to sleep?

HAUPTMANN. Yes, please, let me sleep —

POLICEMAN 2. Why don't you just tell us and then you can sleep.

HAUPTMANN. Tell you what?

POLICEMAN 2. You know what, Bruno.

HAUPTMANN. I have told you.

POLICEMAN 2. Not everything.

HAUPTMANN. Ya, everything.

POLICEMAN 2. Not everything, Bruno.

HAUPTMANN. I have told you the truth!

POLICEMAN 2. You haven't, Bruno.

HAUPTMANN. Ya! The truth!

POLICEMAN 2. Calm down.

HAUPTMANN. You say to me "calm down," and you keep me here all night. I sleep — no, I sleep not — I am too tired to calm myself.

POLICEMAN 2. Bruno, all you have to do is tell us the truth.

HAUPTMANN. Already I have told you the truth.

POLICEMAN 2. You haven't, Bruno.

HAUPTMANN. Only the truth. I know nothing about this.

POLICEMAN 2. Nothing about this?

HAUPTMANN. Nothing.

POLICEMAN 2. You know, Bruno, if you don't tell us the truth we will have to get someone else to tell us.

HAUPTMANN. What do you talk?

POLICEMAN 2. Your wife, Bruno. Anna.

HAUPTMANN. Anna can tell you nothing because she knows nothing —

POLICEMAN 2. You mean you didn't tell her anything?

HAUPTMANN. No -- no, because there is nothing to know!

(Pause. POLICEMAN 2 signals to POLICEMAN 3.)

POLICEMAN 2. Start again.

POLICEMAN 3. Bruno, let's start again, okay? On Tuesday March 1st you were in Hopewell, New Jersey.

HAUPTMANN. No, I didn't even know of Hopewell till after.

POLICEMAN 3. But you'd been there before?

HAUPTMANN. No.

POLICEMAN 3. But you'd been in New Jersey before?

HAUPTMANN. Yes.

POLICEMAN 3. Working on carpentry jobs.

HAUPTMANN. Ya, working on carpentry jobs.

POLICEMAN 3. As a matter of fact didn't you work on the Lindbergh house?

HAUPTMANN. No.

POLICEMAN 3. Well then, you visited the grounds? Met one of the servants?

HAUPTMANN. No, never. I never saw the house. I was never inside the grounds.

POLICEMAN 3. Never met Violet Sharpe?

HAUPTMANN. No — And what about her! What about Violet Sharpe?! She killed herself! Why?!

POLICEMAN 3. Calm down, Bruno.

HAUPTMANN. Did you do this to her too? Did you make her think she was wrong, maybe guilty too —

POLICEMAN 3. Why do you feel guilty, Bruno?

(Pause.)

HAUPTMANN. I do not.

POLICEMAN 3. Honestly, Bruno, it's not going to help you to lie. We know everything. On March 1st you stole the Lindbergh baby from the crib —

HAUPTMANN. No.

POLICEMAN 3. And then you killed him, or dropped him, coming down the ladder —

HAUPTMANN. No. I never saw the baby.

POLICEMAN 3. Sure you did, Richard. You saw him twice. First alive and then dead.

HAUPTMANN. No, you have someone wrong.

POLICEMAN 3. Well, then what were you doing that night?

HAUPTMANN. It was two and a half years ago. I can't remember.

POLICEMAN 3. You can't remember?

HAUPTMANN. Can you remember what you were doing two and a half years ago?

POLICEMAN 3. I wasn't killing a baby.

HAUPTMANN. And neither was I!

(Pause.)

POLICEMAN 1. Hey, pal, ya know what we found in your garage? *(HAUPTMANN is silent.)* We found money, Bruno. Lindbergh ransom money. *(HAUPTMANN is silent.)* We found a lot of money hidden in your garage.

HAUPTMANN. I told you already about that.

POLICEMAN 1. Oh that's right, you did. An old buddy gave it to you —

HAUPTMANN. Isidor Fisch gave it to me when he was leaving for a vacation in Germany. He told me to keep it please for two months. He told me it was important papers.

POLICEMAN 1. Important papers?

HAUPTMANN. Ya.

POLICEMAN 1. *(Smiling.)* I'll say.

HAUPTMANN. He told me to keep it for him safe.

POLICEMAN 1. Isidor Fisch, huh? Well, I suppose we can get in touch with him?

HAUPTMANN. No.

POLICEMAN 1. No? *(Pause.)* And why is that, Bruno?

HAUPTMANN. I told you.

POLICEMAN 1. Oh that's right, we can't get in touch with Isidor Fisch because he died in Germany, right?

HAUPTMANN. He died in Germany, yes.

POLICEMAN 1. *(Laughs.)* Pretty "Fischy" story, Bruno.

HAUPTMANN. Well, yeah, sometimes maybe the truth look like that.

POLICEMAN 1. The "old friend gave it to me" story, eh? *(HAUPTMANN does not respond.)* I do like the death in Europe bit. Lots of imagination.

HAUPTMANN. Isidor Fisch died in Germany of tuberculosis. Check on it.

POLICEMAN 1. We will, sport. You can count on it. *(Pause.)* So this alleged Isidor Fisch left you this money —

HAUPTMANN. I didn't know it was money.

POLICEMAN 1. What did you think was in that box, Bruno? Movie star clippings? *(Policemen laugh.)* Maybe Carole Lombard pictures? *(Pause.)* So you put this shoe box in your closet and didn't think about it until you had a leak in the closet —

HAUPTMANN. Until the box was soaked, yes —

POLICEMAN 1. And it soaked the box and you took it down an— oh boy! — what did you find? *(Pause.)* No pictures of Carole Lombard?

HAUPTMANN. No.

POLICEMAN 1. You found the money.

HAUPTMANN. Yes.

POLICEMAN 1. And whatever did you plan to do with this money?

HAUPTMANN. Give it to Fisch's brother when he came to America.

POLICEMAN 1. What an honest fellow. Not take a bit for your trouble?

HAUPTMANN. Only what he owed me.

POLICEMAN 1. So you felt free to spend what he owed you from business?

HAUPTMANN. I did, yes.

POLICEMAN 1. And that is the money you were spending that was traced to you?

HAUPTMANN. Yes.

POLICEMAN 1. And where did that money come from?

HAUPTMANN. I beg your pardon?

POLICEMAN 1. And where did all that money come from that was in the shoe box?

HAUPTMANN. Isidor Fisch gave —

POLICEMAN 1. And where did the money come from before that?

(Pause.)

HAUPTMANN. From Colonel Lindbergh, I guess.

(Pause.)

POLICEMAN 1. But, heck, you didn't know that, right?

(Pause. POLICEMAN 1 signals for POLICEMAN 2 to take over the interrogation.)

POLICEMAN 2. Bruno.

HAUPTMANN. Ya.

POLICEMAN 2. Have you ever been in Hopewell, New Jersey?

HAUPTMANN. No.

POLICEMAN 2. But you're a carpenter, right?

HAUPTMANN. Yes.

POLICEMAN 2. Could you build, say, a door frame?

HAUPTMANN. Yes.

POLICEMAN 2. A wooden box?

HAUPTMANN. Yes.

POLICEMAN 2. A ladder?

HAUPTMANN. Yes.

POLICEMAN 2. Ever built a ladder?

HAUPTMANN. Once or twice maybe.

POLICEMAN 2. As a matter of fact, didn't you build a ladder and climb into the Lindbergh house and steal that baby?

HAUPTMANN. No.

POLICEMAN 2. And then somehow the baby fell? Or you killed it, right?

HAUPTMANN. No!

POLICEMAN 2. And you stripped off the sleeping suit because you thought you might need it and stuffed the kid into a little hole, didn't you?

HAUPTMANN. No.

POLICEMAN 2. You are a goddamn liar.

HAUPTMANN. I am not.

POLICEMAN 2. You beat the kid over the head and stuffed him into that little hole, didn't you?

HAUPTMANN. No, I never — !

POLICEMAN 2. You bastard. You pervert.

HAUPTMANN. I never saw the Lindbergh baby!

POLICEMAN 2. You are a fucking liar!

HAUPTMANN. I never saw him — !

POLICEMAN 2. *Tell the truth for once!*

HAUPTMANN. *I AM!*

POLICEMAN 2. *TELL THE TRUTH!*

HAUPTMANN. *ALL RIGHT!! (HAUPTMANN bursts from his chair.)* All right! You want to hear a story, I tell you a story. You want to hear? Fine! I'll tell you! *(He lurches forward. The lights begin to dim to a single light on HAUPTMANN as he speaks. He pauses for control and then speaks directly to the audience. He speaks deliberately and darkly.)* You want to hear a story, then listen ...

It was cold on March 1st. He wore a heavy overcoat and his hat pulled down over his eyes. He turned up his collar but still the wind whipped. He drove to New Jersey. He drove to Hopewell. To the Lindbergh house. As he neared the house he shut off his headlights and made his way by moonlight. Everything was blue in the full moon. He turned into the Lindbergh estate and shut off his engine. The car coasted down the long driveway and finally stopped about two hundred feet away from the house. He sat in the car and watched the house. He could see the lights in the windows and feel the cold air. He smoked a cigarette and waited. The light in the nursery window went out.

Finally he opened the car door —- careful to make no noise. He stood by the car and then began slowly walking toward the house. Under one arm he carried a ladder. The other hand was stuffed deep in his coat pocket. The gravel of the driveway crunched under his feet so he tried to step lightly.

He was almost to the house. Taking all the time in the world he advanced to the outside wall of the house and flattened his back against the wall. He could hear the music from the wireless inside. He listened. Then he stepped toward a window and peeked in. Inside a fire was burning. He saw someone move in the corner. His heart froze. Colonel Lindbergh sat reading his paper, content. His long legs were crossed and his feet were warmed by the fire. He watched through the window for some time. So close to such a famous man ...

Finally he turned away from the warm fire and Colonel Lindbergh and made his way around the corner to the side of the house that was home to the nursery window. He looked up and saw only dark ... cold ... glass. He carefully placed the ladder against the house — being sure not to make any noise when it made actual contact with the side of the house.

The ladder in place he paused once more and then began climbing. Some of the rungs bent slightly under his weight as he climbed. When he reached the top he peeked around the corner of the window and into the nursery. All was quiet.

Slowly he worked open the window with a chisel and reached one leg into the room and then the other. He was suddenly inside the house. He heard the sounds of people below and waited. As he waited he became aware of another sound. The soft ... rhythmic ... breathing ... of ... a baby.

He smiled as he listened to the warm sound. His hands sought the sound and discovered the crib, and inside the crib, the baby. Quickly he pulled the baby from the crib and placed the note on the window sill, he looked around the room one last time, gathering it all in. He felt the desire to laugh or sing or something. But silently he carefully stepped through the window onto the ladder. The baby was still asleep on his shoulder. Still the warm breathing continued, only a little louder in his ear.

And then — under his foot a rung snapped. Loudly the crack of wood echoed — he lost his balance and grabbed to stay on the ladder. In doing so the baby slipped from his arms. He made a mad grasp but missed by inches. Forever the baby seemed to tumble through the air. Finally, finally he saw the baby thud against the house and hit the ground. He died then.

The sound of the crack was loud and he climbed down the ladder quickly. He grabbed the ladder in one hand and snatched the baby into his arms. He tried to run across the lawn toward the car but the ladder and the baby were awkward and he felt warmth on his fingers -- he thought of Colonel Lindbergh's fire. He dropped the ladder and looked down at the baby.

He finally reached the car and gently put the baby into the passenger seat and drove away. The baby slumped over in the seat and his blood was dark as it flowed across the seat. In panic he stopped the car, where he was not sure, and dragged the baby after him into the woods.

He found a clearing with a small ditch. Frantically he looked around. But of course it was only silent and cold and lonely. He knelt by the baby and looked at it. It grew paler and paler in the blue light. He looked and thought ... they will want something, proof. Slowly he began to unbutton the sleeping suit.

Then he worked with his hands, strong hands, to cover the baby with leaves. He stood. And the Lindbergh baby lay dead at his feet.

(The lights fade.)

END OF ACT ONE

ACT II

(HAUPTMANN stands still, center-stage. The GUARDS surround him and snap startling, flash pictures of him as we hear various overlapping lines:)

HAWKER. Get 'em here! The one and only Lindbergh kidnap ladder toy! Only ten cents and great for the kids!
LANDLADY. Rooms to rent! A dollar a day including meals. No more room in the hotel! Rooms to rent!
NEWSPAPER BOY. Extra Edition Today! Bruno Goes To Trial! Only a nickel! Extra Edition Today!
VENDOR. Red Hots! Get Your Red Hots! Red Hots and Beer!

(One GUARD steps forward.)

RUNYON. Damon Runyon from Flemington, New Jersey. Today marks the opening day of the Lindbergh kidnapping trial and the air is electric with anticipation. The lawyers and the policemen, the curious and the annoyed scramble to get the best positions in the crowded courtroom —

(Another GUARD steps forward.)

WOOLCOTT. Alexander Woolcott here. Yesterday Flemington, New Jersey was a sleepy little burg that richly deserved its own anonymity. But now capricious fate has thrust innocent Flemington into the jaded eye of the entire nation —

(Another GUARD steps forward.)

EDNA FERBER. Edna Ferber, direct to you from Flemington where the trial of Richard Hauptmann for the kidnap-slaying of little Charlie Lindbergh Jr. is about to commence.

The men of New York have brought their gals from the city as if this were the opening of the newest play on Broadway. Decked out in morning tweeds and flapper furs they crowd the streets of little Flemington, descending from chauffeur driven Rolls Royces to the rural streets below ...

(Another GUARD steps forward as the GUARDS place chairs to create the courtroom.)

MAHAR. Eddie Mahar to you from Flemington, New Jersey. It is the first day of the Hauptmann trial and we are all wondering what *he* is thinking. What goes through his mind as he sees the pre-trial excitement? He looks to me to be what could be expected from a baby killer. His cold grey eyes glare from under thick and knitted brows. His features are sharp and Germanic. He can't help reminding one of the Fuehrer himself.

(The LINDBERGHS enter. The GUARDS race to them and bustle around them like a wolf pack, flashing pictures.)

H. L. MENCKEN. H. L. Mencken from Flemington. Well, folks, this is the biggest story since the Resurrection.

(JUDGE TRENCHARD's gavel raps loudly and the guards quickly step to their seats in the courtroom. JUDGE TRENCHARD takes his chair. Everyone sits after the JUDGE. The BAILIFF stands.)

BAILIFF. The state of New Jersey, Hunterdon County Court of Oyer and Terminer, Holden before the Honorable Judge Thomas W. Trenchard, Justice of the Supreme Court. December term, 1934. To wit: The State of New Jersey versus Bruno Richard Hauptmann. Sur Indictment for murder.

HAUPTMANN. And so I was the Lindbergh kidnapper. All across the world people spoke Lindbergh's name and my name in the same breath. I could feel hate drain from people's eyes as they looked at me. They would point and whisper to their neighbor: "That's him. That's the baby-killer. It must be. Just look at those steely grey eyes."

My eyes are blue.

The prosecuting attorney was a very smart man named David Wilentz. He is dangerous. He smokes long cigars. My attorney was a man named Edward J. Reilly. He is a very famous New York lawyer who is well known for his dramatic pleadings before the jury — a New York jury anyway. In Flemington his spats and fresh buttonhole seemed an insult. Mr. Reilly was known by the disquieting appellation of "Death-House Reilly" for his marked lack of success in capital punishment cases. I couldn't talk to "Death-House" the day my trial began, unfortunately. He was still drunk from a New Year's party the day before. *(The court stirs to attention as WILENTZ stands and walks back and forth speaking in low tones. Only snatches of what he is saying are heard through HAUPTMANN's dialogue.)* In New Jersey law only the State is allowed to make an opening statement. It is supposed to be a brief summation of the facts of the case. But of course in a case like mine the facts can be seen through differing eyes.

WILENTZ. And then the defendant climbed into the house and ripped the sleeping infant from the crib ...

HAUPTMANN. It was fascinating to watch Mr. Wilentz talk about me. He spoke as if he hated me. As if I frightened him.

WILENTZ. And on the way down the ladder are we to assume that the baby fell ... ?

HAUPTMANN. I haunt Mr. Wilentz.

WILENTZ. Not satisfied with that, he peeled off the bloody sleeping suit and pushed ...

HAUPTMANN. Finally I couldn't watch him anymore. I turned away and tried to find Anna's face in the crowd but I only saw strangers. They all sat looking at Wilentz. No one was looking at me. Then someone shifted out of the way and I saw that one person was looking at me. Colonel Lindbergh sat watching me. His eyes were sharp as they studied me. This was the first time I had been face to face with him. The Lone Eagle watching the Lone Wolf ...

WILENTZ. After collecting the money from Dr. Condon, the defendant fled into the night with his bounty ...

HAUPTMANN.Then, slowly ... Lindbergh smiled at me. I could not understand. Then he dropped his eyes to his jacket and looked back at me. My eyes followed his and I realized that he was wearing a revolver in a shoulder holster. He smiled at me.

WILENTZ. And then why was the money in his garage? Where did he get it?

HAUPTMANN. Lindbergh's eyes are grey.

WILENTZ. For my first witness I would like to call Anne Morrow Lindbergh to the stand. *(ANNE LINDBERGH goes to the witness chair.)* Mrs. Lindbergh, you are the wife of Colonel Charles Lindbergh.

ANNE LINDBERGH. I am.

WILENTZ. And where do you reside?

ANNE LINDBERGH. I have been living in Englewood, New Jersey.

WILENTZ. Will you please tell us, on the first day of March in 1932, who were the occupants of your home in Hopewell?

ANNE LINDBERGH. I was there and my son, Charles Lindbergh Jr., the Whatleys, Betty Gow, Violet Sharpe and my husband.

WILENTZ. How old was your son?

ANNE LINDBERGH. Twenty months.

WILENTZ. Now, during the day of March 1st, did you play with your son?

ANNE LINDBERGH. I was with him all morning. I put him down for his nap about one in the afternoon and I played with him when he awoke from his nap.

WILENTZ. At what other time did you see your baby on that day?

ANNE LINDBERGH. Well, just before supper I took a little walk around the house and threw a pebble up at his window and the nurse, Betty Gow, held him up at the window for me to see.

WILENTZ. She held him up at the window?

ANNE LINDBERGH. Yes.

WILENTZ. Did he recognize you?

ANNE LINDBERGH. Yes. He waved.

WILENTZ. Was he a normal child?

ANNE LINDBERGH. He was perfectly normal.

WILENTZ. Playful?

ANNE LINDBERGH. Oh, yes.

WILENTZ. Was he able to talk?

ANNE LINDBERGH. He talked.

WILENTZ. To what extent, Mrs. Lindbergh?

ANNE LINDBERGH. I don't remember any particular conversations on that afternoon. But he called all the members of the household by their names, and he played on the floor in the living room with me and ... um ... talked to his stuffed animals.

WILENTZ. Will you tell us, please, the color of his hair?

ANNE LINDBERGH. It was light golden.

WILENTZ. I'm sorry, Mrs. Lindbergh, would you speak up a bit?

ANNE LINDBERGH. His hair was light golden.

WILENTZ. Thank you. And the color of his eyes, please?

ANNE LINDBERGH. Blue.

HAUPTMANN. Mrs. Lindbergh seemed very different than in the newsreels. I saw only a smallish woman whose hands pulled at a little handkerchief. Her voice was very small. And she did not glimmer.

WILENTZ. Mrs. Lindbergh, when was the last time you saw your baby?

ANNE LINDBERGH. It was about six-fifteen on the evening of March 1st. I stayed with him until he was ready for bed. He had been dressed and given the medicine for his cold, a lotion ...

WILENTZ. Vick's vapor rub?

ANNE LINDBERGH. Yes, for his cold.

WILENTZ. And at about what time did you leave the nursery?

ANNE LINDBERGH. About seven-thirty.

WILENTZ. And you did not see your child after you left the nursery? *(Pause.)* Oh, I'm sorry, you did not see your child alive after you left the nursery.

ANNE LINDBERGH. I did not.

(Pause.)

WILENTZ: To the best of your ability, Mrs. Lindbergh, would

you describe the rest of the night's activities?

ANNE LINDBERGH. I went downstairs after I put Charles Jr. to bed and waited for my husband to return from the city. He had called to say that he would be a bit late. When he returned we had dinner and then we went into the study to talk for a little while. Then my husband went to take a bath while I read. After he had bathed he went to the library to read and I prepared for bed. I was brushing my hair when Betty Gow, the baby's nurse, came into my bedroom and asked if the baby was with me. *(Pause.)* I checked the crib while she got my husband. We could not find Charles Jr. My husband telephoned the police.

(She is silent.)

WILENTZ. Thank you, you may step down Mrs. Lindbergh.

(She rises and returns to her seat in the courtroom.)

HAUPTMANN. She did not glimmer.... As she walked slowly up the crowded aisle in the courtroom I asked myself the same questions I had asked myself two years before when I opened the newspaper to read that the Lindbergh baby had been taken: who could do such a thing? What kind of man? Who? And where is he now?

WILENTZ. I would like to call Albert Osborne to the stand.

(ALBERT OSBORNE, an elderly handwriting analyst, steps forward and takes the stand as HAUPTMANN speaks.)

HAUPTMANN. I should explain to you that I was not paying the salary of my attorney, Mr. Reilly. He was being paid by the Hearst newspapers, which wanted exclusive rights to my story. So they paid for Mr. Reilly to defend me. We also had no money for experts.

Most of the prosecution's case was built on these expert witnesses who were brought in and paid to say I was the killer. These people were engaged to render an opinion. They came and talked about everything. They talked about the wood from the ladder, about my carpentry, about my mental state, about my bank account. And my defense had no money to pay for so many expert witnesses like these. So the jury heard it from the prosecution. For my defense we were only able to raise $4,000. The prosecution spent over a million.

OSBORNE. *(Refers to specimens of Hauptmann's handwriting:)* Of course you will see the "y" is not only made like the "j" but you will observe, if you look veerrryyy carefully, that the stroke of the letter is curved to the right, the downward stroke, look — that's it — uh, no — well — over there then — Yes — uhm — and it is my opinion that the freedom of these letters indicates that they were in fact not imitations but they do vary slightly to suggest that they were written — um — quickly.

HAUPTMANN. For *days* he went on about it.

OSBORNE. Now there are statements in these letters which, in my opinion, tend to connect them with each other and, especially, with the latter letter — that is the ladder letter, not the latter, but we'll get to that letter later — where is it? There, sure, that's it. Anyway, it proves that the letters are all connected with the first ransom note. The first letter says: "the baby is in gut care." Now that particular sentence was written with a coarser pen —

HAUPTMANN. He went on and on. He might as well have stopped with a few words: "Mr. Wilentz: Are you saying that all the ransom notes were written by the same hand and that the handwriting matches the handwriting of the defendant? Mr. Osborne: Uh — yes, that is correct." You must understand that handwriting analysis is about as empirical and exact as reading tea-leaves. It is a subjective judgement only —

WILENTZ. Thank you, Mr. Osborne, that will be all. I would like to call Mr. Arthur Koehler to the stand.

(KOEHLER, another elderly expert, is sworn in as HAUPTMANN speaks.)

HAUPTMANN. They called in expert after expert to say that I had done it. The handwriting was mine, they said. And the wood from the kidnap ladder came from my own attic!

WILENTZ. Mr. Koehler, you say that the left-hand Southern pine side rail of the kidnap ladder has been compared to some of the wood in Richard Hauptmann's attic?

KOEHLER. It has.

WILENTZ. And what relationship did you find between the ladder rail and the wood in Hauptmann's attic?

KOEHLER. They were identical.

(HAUPTMANN starts.)

WILENTZ. So you can testify that the side rail from the kidnap ladder came from the defendant's attic?

HAUPTMANN. Mr. Reilly rose to speak in my defense ... *(HAUPTMANN stands.)* Allow me to present Mr. Reilly's defense:

I object, Your Honor! If the witness says that there is any relationship between the side rail of the kidnap ladder and some wood in Hauptmann's attic he is only expressing an opinion. And in my view he is not qualified to express such an opinion.

JUDGE TRENCHARD. Do you say that the witness doesn't qualify as an expert on wood?

HAUPTMANN. I say that there is no such animal as an expert on wood. Wood technology, you see, is not an exact science and cannot be recognized in court in the same class as fingerprint experts, ballistic experts — or even handwriting experts.

WILENTZ. You might have raised your objection when the expert was being introduced!

HAUPTMANN. How did I know he was going to make irresponsible claims?

WILENTZ. If you think —

JUDGE TRENCHARD. Gentlemen! Mr. Reilly, I think the witness is very well qualified as an expert on the *exact* science of wood analysis.

(HAUPTMANN sits.)

WILENTZ. Now, Mr. Koehler, if we can finally get back to that attic wood. What makes you think that the rail you got from Hauptmann's attic floor was at one time connected to the side rail of the kidnap ladder?

KOEHLER. The nail holes all match up in size, impression, density and depth. The same square nails were used on both sides of this one piece of wood. Also the grain runs pretty evenly from the attic board to the ladder board. And the knot hole in the missing section seems to suggest —

HAUPTMANN. *(Rises as REILLY)* Excuse me, your honor, what "missing section"?

WILENTZ. Mr. Reilly — !

KOEHLER. I speak of a piece of wood an inch and a quarter long that seems to be missing when the two pieces of wood are put together —

HAUPTMANN. Your Honor, I object to this witness basing his testimony on a piece of wood that does not exist!

WILENTZ. Now hold on —

HAUPTMANN. You could take almost any two pieces of Southern pine showing the same general grain and manipulate them enough to get a rough match —

JUDGE TRENCHARD. Over-ruled.

(HAUPTMANN sits.)

WILENTZ. Mr. Koehler, yesterday you were talking about a certain chisel. *(He walks to the evidence table and returns with a chisel.)* Now, Mr. Koehler, is this one of the tools that was used to build the kidnap ladder?

KOEHLER. Well, I couldn't be a million per cent sure, but it was evident that a three-quarter inch chisel, much like this one in specifications, was used to build the kidnap ladder.

WILENTZ. I would like the jury to note that this chisel was found on the grounds of the Lindbergh estate —

HAUPTMANN. *(Rises as REILLY)* I object to your insinuation! For the witness to say that an ordinary three-quarter inch chisel was used to make the kidnap ladder does not connect it with this particular chisel in any way. That is obvious.

JUDGE TRENCHARD. Well, perhaps it is a circumstance for the jury to consider.

HAUPTMANN. It might be if the chisel was found in

Hauptmann's garage or tool box, but in fact it was found some forty miles from there —

JUDGE TRENCHARD. It was found under the room where the ransom note was left — and that note has been traced to the defendant.

HAUPTMANN. *(Stiffens)* We don't agree to that!

JUDGE TRENCHARD. I am only telling what the evidence tends to show. Therefore, I think the pieces of circumstance must be given over to the jury for consideration. That is my ruling on the matter.

(HAUPTMANN sits in defeat. WILENTZ continues to examine KOEHLER as HAUPTMANN speaks to the audience.)

HAUPTMANN. For days turning into weeks I sat as the witnesses were brought up against me. They said I had written Dr. Condon's telephone number on my kitchen door. I had not. They said I had spent ransom money long before Isidor Fisch gave it to me. Of course, I had not. Mr. Koehler said that one day he discovered a short rail in my attic floor that matched one of the side rails of the kidnap ladder. My question is: why didn't anyone notice it earlier? Over nine different police, FBI detective patrols scoured my attic. Over thirty-eight different policemen made complete reports on my attic and not one mentions this obviously shorter rail? Then, all of a sudden, out of nowhere, Mr. Koehler noticed it. And what do you know, the side rail from the ladder fits perfectly into the space provided — that is if you don't notice the inch and a quarter gap between the two boards!

It was faked. If I am the master criminal Mr. Wilentz says I am, then why would I choose wood from my own attic to build the ladder? It does not make sense.

(As he speaks AMANDUS HOCHMUTH, a withered old man, is sworn in.)

And through these weeks I kept my patience. I would not show my pain. I kept it all in — until one day Mr. Wilentz was questioning an ancient creature named Amandus Hochmuth who swore that he saw me driving past his house on the day of the kidnapping.

WILENTZ. And how far do you live from the Lindbergh house?

HOCHMUTH. Well, about twenty yards up the road.

WILENTZ. Will you tell us if anything unusual happened on the evening of March 1st, 1932?

HOCHMUTH. Sure enough, I was a sittin' on my front porch which looks over the main road that led to the Lindbergh place. When I see a car comin' round the corner, pretty good speed, and I figure it's gonna turn over in the ditch. And, as the car was about twenty-five feet away from me, the driver in the car was lookin' out the window like this — *(He imitates a devilish glare.)* And he glared like he seen a ghost.

WILENTZ. The man you saw, is he in this room?

HOCHMUTH. Yes.

WILENTZ. Would you please get up and touch him on the shoulder.

(HOCHMUTH rises and slowly advances on HAUPTMANN. When he finally grabs HAUPTMANN's shoulder, HAUPTMANN suddenly stands and shouts.)

HAUPTMANN. *Dieser alter ist verruckt* — this old man is crazy! He is telling a story. Mister, you tell the truth!

(ANNA pulls HAUPTMANN down as HOCHMUTH returns to the stand.)

WILENTZ. Your witness, Mr. Reilly.

(HAUPTMANN stands as REILLY.)

HAUPTMANN. Mr. Hochmuth, haven't you seen Richard Hauptmann's picture in the newspapers?

HOCHMUTH. I suppose I might have done.

HAUPTMANN. And didn't a state trooper point him out to you when you entered the courtroom? *(No answer.)* As a matter of fact, isn't your eyesight very poor? Your mind inclined to wander?

HOCHMUTH. Well ...

HAUPTMANN. How far from your front porch was the man in the car?

HOCHMUTH. About fifty feet.

HAUPTMANN. But didn't you just say twenty-five feet a moment ago?

HOCHMUTH. Did I?

HAUPTMANN. You certainly did.

WILENTZ. The witness is being badgered —

HAUPTMANN. How would you describe the man in the car? What was he wearing?

HOCHMUTH. I ain't sure.

HAUPTMANN. Was he wearing a hat?

HOCHMUTH. I ain't sure. All I remember was that red face and them glaring eyes.

HAUPTMANN. A red face.

HOCHMUTH. Yes! Very red.

HAUPTMANN. *(Turning to AUDIENCE)* Look at my face now. In the newspapers I have heard my face described as "sallow," "pale," "jaundiced" and even "cadaverous"! But hardly *red*! *(Pause.)* I remember one of the first stories my prison guards told me about the trial. One of the guards had been stationed with Mr. Wilentz when Mr. Hochmuth came in for an interview. As Mr. Wilentz was talking to him he began to realize that Mr. Hochmuth's eyesight was very poor indeed. In fact, Mr. Hochmuth admitted, on his last driving test he had been declared *legally blind*. Wilentz pointed to a filing cabinet with a vase of flowers on it and asked the old man to identify it. The old man looked and looked and finally decided that it was a woman wearing a very becoming hat. The guards laughed at that. *(Pause.)*

The next witness was Dr. John F. Condon.

(CONDON is on the stand being examined by WILENTZ.)

WILENTZ. In St. Raymond's cemetery you met a man called John and you gave him a wooden box containing the Lindbergh ransom money. Is that correct?

CONDON. Absolutely correct.

WILENTZ. Who did you give the money to?

CONDON. I gave it to John.

WILENTZ. Dr. Condon, who is John?

CONDON. John is Bruno Richard Hauptmann!

WILENTZ. Your witness, Mr. Reilly.

(HAUPTMANN, as REILLY, rises sharply to cross examine.)

HAUPTMANN. Dr. Condon, you have been questioned by the police several times, you have seen line-ups of suspects -- including the defendant -- and yet you have never made a positive identification that Richard Hauptmann is John. What — or who — changed your mind?

CONDON. I object to your tone, sir.

HAUPTMANN. I object to your lying, sir.

CONDON. I have never told a lie in my life.

HAUPTMANN. You have never told any policeman or federal agents or any FBI men that Hauptmann is John, have you?

CONDON. I have never discussed it in public, and I neither affirmed nor denied it. I make a definite distinction between "identification" and "declaration of identification."

HAUPTMANN. Am I to understand, sir, with a man's life in the balance you are splitting hairs in words?

CONDON. No hairs at all. I want to be honest.

HAUPTMANN. In the Greenwich Village police station you said that it was not the man.

CONDON. No, sir, I did not.

HAUPTMANN. Well, you never said it was the man.

CONDON. I never said it was or was not.

HAUPTMANN. Because you were not sure.

CONDON. Because I make a distinction between "declaration" and "identification." Identification means what I know mentally, the declaration means what I say to others.

HAUPTMANN. Were you not brought there for the purpose of *identifying* John?

CONDON. I was, yes.

HAUPTMANN. And you didn't *identify* him, did you?

CONDON. I must take exception to your language once again. When you divide the identification and the declaration, you make it appear that I was dishonest, and I am not! Is that too severe, Judge?

JUDGE TRENCHARD. *(Caught off guard)* Uh — no.

HAUPTMANN. No more questions. You may step down.

(HAUPTMANN returns to his chair.)

WILENTZ, I would like to call Colonel Charles Lindbergh to the stand. *(LINDBERGH stands and briskly walks to the witness chair.)* Colonel Lindbergh, on the night of March 1st, 1932, you returned from your work at about seven thirty. Is that correct?

LINDBERGH. It is, yes.

WILENTZ. Would you tell us, briefly, your actions when you returned home?

LINDBERGH. Well, it was a cold night so the first thing I did upon entering the house was request that a fire be lit. Then I went upstairs and met my wife and I looked in on my son.

(ANNA HAUPTMANN stands.)

ANNA. Richard came home from work a little early that night because he was going to help get the house ready for our friends.

LINDBERGH. I went in and pulled the covers a little closer around the child and then Anne and I went downstairs to dinner. We ate and talked about the days events.

ANNA. We cleaned the house quickly, then I put some baked goods I had bought into the oven. Rolls and cookies. We were having friends over.

LINDBERGH. We ate alone and then retired to the study where we talked some more and warmed ourselves by the fire. Anne was a bit cold so I had one of the servants fetch her a quilt. She, I remember, was feeling much better about the child's cold and felt Charles Jr. would be much better by morning.

ANNA. The whole house smelled of warm baking.

LINDBERGH. I talked to her about seeing a doctor if she caught the child's cold.

ANNA. When our friends arrived we all went in and looked at Manfred who was asleep. They all cooed over him and wanted to pick him up. Richard laughed, but I refused to let anyone wake him. He slept very soundly.

LINDBERGH. Anne noted that Charles Jr. was sleeping much better since she had been coating his chest with the vapor rub. She thought that perhaps the nursery was a little drafty because of the broken shutters and I promised to have them looked at soon.

ANNA. After we left Manfred we went into our living room and sang and played songs from Germany. Richard played on his mandolin and our good friend Hans Kloeppenburg played on his guitar.

LINDBERGH. I then took a bath and went into the library to read. I sat in front of the fire.

ANNA. And then I served the cookies and we all sang.

LINDBERGH. Anne was upstairs getting ready for bed and I listened to the wireless for a while.

ANNA. I remember we all argued about the rise of the National Socialists and Hans thought it would be bad for our families left in Germany.

LINDBERGH. I did not hear or see anything outside the window.

ANNA. Richard said he thought they would be safe.

LINDBERGH. I read a bit more and then Betty Gow came running into the library —

ANNA. We played a few more songs and argued some more and then they left and we cleaned up.

LINDBERGH. She told me that Charles Jr. was missing.

ANNA. We checked on Manfred once more.

LINDBERGH. I ran upstairs and checked the crib ... which was empty. Anne was in tears and I tried to comfort her.

ANNA. He slept soundly.

LINDBERGH. Then I noticed the letter on the window sill. I called the police.

ANNA. And we went to sleep.

LINDBERGH. And that is what happened on March 1st, 1932.

ANNA. *That is all.*

(Pause. ANNE sits. WILENTZ steps to LINDBERGH.)

WILENTZ. Colonel Lindbergh, on April 2nd of 1932 you accompanied Dr. John F. Condon to a secluded part of the Bronx near St. Raymond's cemetery. Isn't that right?

LINDBERGH. Yes, that is correct.

WILENTZ. And about how long did you wait when you got to the cemetery?

LINDBERGH. For about an hour.

WILENTZ. And then someone called out to you?

LINDBERGH. Yes, a voice came from inside the cemetery.

WILENTZ. And what did the voice say?

LINDBERGH. In an accent, "Hey Doctor ... hey Doctor, over here."

WILENTZ. And did you ever hear that voice again?

LINDBERGH. I did.

WILENTZ. And where was that?

LINDBERGH. In a police station in Greenwich Village.

WILENTZ. And whose voice was it?

LINDBERGH. It was Hauptmann's voice.

ANNA. *(Whispers:)* You lie.

WILENTZ. And you have no doubt about that?

LINDBERGH. None what so ever.

ANNA. You lie ...

(LINDBERGH leaves the stand. HAUPTMANN steps forward and speaks to the audience.)

HAUPTMANN. That was over three years ago! Thirty-six months and he claims that he can remember four words called out on a windy night. He can recognize that voice and claim it was mine with no doubt *"what so ever"*! Three years!

WILENTZ. I will now call Bruno Richard Hauptmann to the stand.

HAUPTMANN. And in all that time he identifies no one — makes no comment about the voice. But once the FBI has traced Isidor Fisch's money to me, Lindbergh is sure it was me!

WILENTZ. I will now call Bruno Richard Hauptmann to the stand.

HAUPTMANN. No reporters mentioned his revolver! No one mentioned the money being spent on the prosecution that I didn't have for my defense. No one mentioned that Amandus Hochmuth is legally blind! Or that Mr. Koehler invented wood to fit my attic! Why does no one write of this? Is the truth not so interesting? Not so interesting because it could save the baby-killer?!

WILENTZ. Bruno Richard Hauptmann, please take the stand. *(HAUPTMANN turns and marches firmly to the witness chair. Long pause as he and WILENTZ stare at each other.)* Mr. Defendant, you came into this country illegally, did you not?

HAUPTMANN. Yes, sir.

WILENTZ. And you have been in the United States since 1923, haven't you?

HAUPTMANN. Yes.

WILENTZ. You have enjoyed the privilege and opportunity of earning a livelihood, haven't you?

HAUPTMANN. Yes, sir.

WILENTZ. And you have received police protection during those years, haven't you?

HAUPTMANN. Not quite.

WILENTZ. Not quite?

HAUPTMANN. Not recently, sir.

WILENTZ. You know, of course, that the State of New Jersey, the State of New York and the United States of America have all been working on your case, you know that don't you?

HAUPTMANN. I suppose so.

WILENTZ. And you have had the opportunity in this court, and you still have the opportunity — right now — this moment — to tell the truth.

HAUPTMANN. I have told the truth already.

WILENTZ. So you stand on the story of your friend Isidor Fisch who left you a box which contained some of the Lindbergh ransom money?

HAUPTMANN. Yes.

WILENTZ. This Isidor Fisch, he was your best friend, wasn't he?

HAUPTMANN. Well, I don't say best friend, but —

WILENTZ. You don't say so?

HAUPTMANN. He was a good friend.

WILENTZ. Did he help you kidnap the Lindbergh child?

HAUPTMANN. I never saw —

WILENTZ. You never saw?

HAUPTMANN. Mrs. Lindbergh's child.

WILENTZ. How do you suppose this Fisch got the money?

HAUPTMANN. I only wish I could ask him —

WILENTZ. So this friend of yours gave you a shoe box full of papers when he left for a vacation in Germany?

HAUPTMANN. Yes.

WILENTZ. And when you had a leak in your closet you moved the box and you discovered it was filled with money?

HAUPTMANN. Yes.

WILENTZ. Let me ask you, how did you feel when you found the $14,000?

HAUPTMANN. How did I feel?

WILENTZ. How did you feel? Did you cry? Did you laugh? Were you happy or sad?

HAUPTMANN. I was excited.

WILENTZ. You were excited?

HAUPTMANN. I was.

WILENTZ. Did you say anything? Did you holler out, "Anna, look what I found!"? Anything like that?

HAUPTMANN. I did not.

WILENTZ. Did you tell your wife?

HAUPTMANN. I did not.

WILENTZ. You didn't tell your wife?

HAUPTMANN. No.

WILENTZ. Well, when you say you were excited, just what do you mean?

HAUPTMANN. Well, I guess everybody is excited if he finds $14,000.

WILENTZ. Yes?

HAUPTMANN. Sure.

WILENTZ. Well, you're not so excited now, are you?

HAUPTMANN. What — why should I?

WILENTZ. No, it's quite a joke with you, isn't it?

HAUPTMANN. No, it is not a joke, I am very earnest.

WILENTZ. Oh, I see. Were you earnest with your wife when you found the $14,000?

HAUPTMANN. That has got nothing to do with my wife.

WILENTZ. Didn't she work and slave in a bakery so that when you were married she could bring all her savings to you?

HAUPTMANN. That has nothing to do with the $14,000.

WILENTZ. Didn't she do that? Answer the question.

HAUPTMANN. Yes.

WILENTZ. She gave you every dollar she had in the world, didn't she?

HAUPTMANN. So did I.

WILENTZ. Yes?

HAUPTMANN. Except the $14,000.

WILENTZ. Oh, I see. You were partners working hard together until you found the $14,000?

HAUPTMANN. Except the $14,000. Yes.

WILENTZ. When you found the $14,000 — no more partnership!

HAUPTMANN. Absolutely not. Why should I make my wife excited about it?

WILENTZ. Why on earth did you hide it from her?

HAUPTMANN. Should it be a pleasant surprise for her sometime.

WILENTZ. You were keeping it for a surprise?

HAUPTMANN. Ya.

(Pause as WILENTZ looks at HAUPTMANN, finally he smiles and shakes his head. WILENTZ goes to the evidence table and brings a small black notebook to HAUPTMANN.)

WILENTZ. Now, I want to show you this little book and ask you if it is yours. Isn't that your handwriting? *(He hands the book to HAUPTMANN.)* Take your time, look at it.

HAUPTMANN. Yes, that's my handwriting.

WILENTZ. Take a look at this word particularly. Tell me if that is your handwriting. That one word there. *(He points. HAUPTMANN does not respond.)* Or did some policeman write it?

HAUPTMANN. I can't remember every word I put in there.

WILENTZ. Just one word, that's all. There are only a few words on the whole page. That one word, is that your handwriting?

HAUPTMANN. It looks like my handwriting. But I can't remember I ever put it there.

WILENTZ. Just say the word aloud please. You see that word?

HAUPTMANN. Yes.

WILENTZ. What is the word?

HAUPTMANN. Boat.

WILENTZ. Now, tell me, how do you spell the word "boat"?

HAUPTMANN. B-O-A-T.

WILENTZ. Yes? But why did you spell it "B-O-A-*D*"?

HAUPTMANN. You wouldn't mind telling me how old this book is?

WILENTZ. I don't know how old it is. Why do you spell boat "B-O-A-D"?

HAUPTMANN. This book is probably eight years old.

WILENTZ. Fine. Why did you spell it "B-O-A-D"?

HAUPTMANN. I was just learning. After you make improvements in your writing —

WILENTZ. All right, so at one time you spelled boat "B-O-A-D'? Didn't you?

HAUPTMANN. No, I don't think so.

WILENTZ. Listen, this isn't a joke. Six, eight, ten years ago, whenever it was, you spelled boat "B-O-A-D." Isn't that so?

HAUPTMANN. I don't know.

WILENTZ. You spelled it there, didn't you?

HAUPTMANN. I ...

WILENTZ. You tell the truth, didn't you spell it there?

HAUPTMANN. Now listen, I can't remember if I put it there.

(WILENTZ gets a letter from the evidence table.)

WILENTZ. The reason you don't remember is because you *know* you wrote "boad" when you got the ransom money from Dr. Condon, isn't that right?

HAUPTMANN. No, sir.

WILENTZ. "Boad Nelly." Look at it. *(He hands the letter to HAUPTMANN.)* Do you see the words "Boad Nelly"?

HAUPTMANN. I see them, certainly.

WILENTZ. Same spelling as in your book?

HAUPTMANN. I don't ...

WILENTZ. Same spelling as in your book?

HAUPTMANN. Same spelling.

(Pause.)

WILENTZ. Mr. Defendant, do you remember the testimony of the handwriting expert about putting extra "n's" in certain words. Do you remember that?

HAUPTMANN. There was so much ... Yes, I remember that.

WILENTZ. That's a habit of yours, isn't it? Putting the "n's" where they don't belong.

HAUPTMANN. No.

WILENTZ. You do it often, don't you?

HAUPTMANN. I can't remember doing it at all.

WILENTZ. Well, look at this for a moment. *(He hands HAUPTMANN a piece of paper from the evidence table.)* Is that your check?

HAUPTMANN. Yes.

WILENTZ. How much is the amount of the check?

HAUPTMANN. Seventy four dollars.

WILENTZ. Seventy four dollars?

HAUPTMANN. Yes.

WILENTZ. How do you spell "seventy"?

HAUPTMANN. "Seventy"? I guess —

WILENTZ. No, read from the check please. You wrote it there. Read it. Nice and loud please.

HAUPTMANN. This is —

WILENTZ. Loud, now.

HAUPTMANN. S-E-

WILENTZ. Louder please, S-E- what?

HAUPTMANN. S-E-N-

WILENTZ. S-E-*N*?

HAUPTMANN. Yes.

WILENTZ. S-E-*N*-V-E-N-T-Y?

HAUPTMANN. Yes.

WILENTZ. You've put an extra "n" in there, haven't you?

HAUPTMANN. Yes.

WILENTZ. The same extra "n" that you put in the word "si*n*gnature," isn't that right?

HAUPTMANN. I--

WILENTZ. *(Quickly:)* How do you spell "signature"?

HAUPTMANN. S-I-N-

WILENTZ. See, that's a tricky one —

HAUPTMANN. S-I-G-N-A-T-U-R-E.

(WILENTZ reads from the ransom note.)

WILENTZ. "And all notes will have this si*n*gnature ..." *(WILENTZ pauses, smiling at HAUPTMANN. He slowly walks to the evidence table, drops the ransom note on it, and returns.)* Mr. Hauptmann, before you came to America you were convicted in Germany in 1919, were you not?

HAUPTMANN. Convicted in 1919 and paroled in 1923.

WILENTZ. So you served four years in Germany?

HAUPTMANN. Four years, ya.

WILENTZ. You were caught trying to sell some stolen goods which you didn't realize were stolen, isn't that right?

HAUPTMANN. Um, yes.

WILENTZ. After you were paroled from this crime, then what happened? Did you go back to jail?

HAUPTMANN. I got arrested.

WILENTZ. And went back to jail again, isn't that right?

HAUPTMANN. It was like a police station really, not a jail.

WILENTZ. All right, and how long did you stay this time?

HAUPTMANN. Only a couple of days.

WILENTZ. Only a couple of days? What happened?

HAUPTMANN. They were working out in the yard and I went out. The door was open and everything ...

WILENTZ. You escaped?

HAUPTMANN. Ya.

WILENTZ. You mean you were paroled for one crime and then ten days later you were arrested again?

HAUPTMANN. That's right.

WILENTZ. Well, you didn't give them a chance to convict you again, you ran away.

HAUPTMANN. That's right. I ran away.

WILENTZ. So you mean you were convicted only once?

HAUPTMANN. Only convicted once.

WILENTZ. Only once?

HAUPTMANN. Yes, sir.

(Pause.)

WILENTZ. But isn't it a fact that on March of the same year you were convicted of a third crime? Of breaking and entering?

HAUPTMANN. It was a charge not convicted.

WILENTZ. You were convicted of breaking and entering into the Mayor's house on March 15th, 1919.

HAUPTMANN. That's about right. I can't remember.

WILENTZ. Breaking in through a second story window — you went through a second story window, didn't you?

HAUPTMANN. Yes.

(Pause.)

WILENTZ. So in Germany, before you came to this country, you were convicted of three crimes?

HAUPTMANN. Not convicted of three —

WILENTZ. You were charged with only these three crimes?

HAUPTMANN. Ya.

WILENTZ. These three?

HAUPTMANN. Ya.

(WILENTZ pauses. He feigns a puzzled look.)

WILENTZ. Oh, but Mr. Hauptmann, I also have listed that you were also charged with another crime. Isn't it a fact that you were also

charged, you and another man, of holding up two women with a gun?
HAUPTMANN. It is.
WILENTZ. Two women wheeling a baby carriage!
HAUPTMANN. Everybody wheels baby carriages!
WILENTZ. Everybody wheels baby carriages and you and this other man with a gun held up these two women wheeling baby carriages, didn't you!?

(HAUPTMANN does not answer. Finally.)

HAUPTMANN. I object to that question.
WILENTZ. You have already answered the question.

(Pause as WILENTZ goes to the evidence table. HAUPTMANN turns to the audience.)

HAUPTMANN. *(Quickly, to AUDIENCE:)* Forgive me for not telling you about that — I should have told you but ...
It happened so long ago, and times were so bad in Germany after the war, people starving everywhere, I did crazy things. So did everybody. I should have told you but since I got to this country I have had no crimes, not even a traffic violation. Please —

(He is interrupted as WILENTZ returns from the evidence table.)

WILENTZ. Mr. Defendant, I'm going to ask you a few questions about your trial in the Bronx. You remember, the extradition hearing before you came here?
HAUPTMANN. Okay.
WILENTZ. In that hearing you said you were never in the Lindbergh house.
HAUPTMANN. That's right.
WILENTZ. You never went there and took the child out of the nursery?
HAUPTMANN. No, sir.
WILENTZ. You never dropped the chisel outside the nursery window?
HAUPTMANN. I was never —

WILENTZ. You never took the ladder there?

HAUPTMANN. I didn't even build the ladder.

WILENTZ. And you didn't collect the $50,000?

HAUPTMANN. No.

WILENTZ. And you never wrote Dr. Condon's telephone number on your kitchen door?

HAUPTMANN. Positively not.

WILENTZ. Positively not?

HAUPTMANN. Positively not.

WILENTZ. Let me read one of your answers from that extradition hearing: "Question: How did you come to put that telephone number on your closet door? Answer: I can't give you any explanation about that number. I was probably reading a newspaper in the kitchen and I just happened to mark it down. Sometimes I write on that door numbers and such."

You told the attorney in that hearing that you probably wrote it down absent-mindedly. Didn't you say that?

HAUPTMANN. I did.

WILENTZ. Is there anything you want to add to your answer?

HAUPTMANN. Well — I can't —- I can't remember I ever wrote —

WILENTZ. So you lied then?

HAUPTMANN. No — I —

WILENTZ. You just said that you had "positively not" written Dr. Condon's telephone number on your closet door. In the Bronx courtroom you said that you had done so. Make up your mind —

HAUPTMANN. No, you are going too fast. You see I think in German and must translate into English.

WILENTZ. When you were arrested they found some gold certificate money in your wallet, did they not?

HAUPTMANN. Ya.

WILENTZ. And when they asked if you had anymore gold certificate bills you said no, is that right?

HAUPTMANN. That is right.

WILENTZ. But that wasn't true either, was it?

HAUPTMANN. It was not.

WILENTZ. No. And when they found all that other gold certificate money in your garage what did you say? *(HAUPTMANN is silent.)* When they found those first Lindbergh bills in your wallet and asked you if you had anymore gold certificate bills, you didn't tell them the truth, and you knew you weren't telling the truth, isn't that right?

HAUPTMANN. That is right.

WILENTZ. Good Lord! Don't you tell the truth to anyone?

HAUPTMANN. I try to!

WILENTZ. This is funny to you, isn't it? You're having a lot of —

HAUPTMANN. No. Absolutely not.

WILENTZ. You're having a lot of fun with me, aren't you?

HAUPTMANN. No.

WILENTZ. Well, you're doing very well, smiling at me every five minutes.

HAUPTMANN. No — Should I cry?

WILENTZ. You think you're a big shot, don't you?

HAUPTMANN. No.

WILENTZ. You think you're bigger than everybody, don't you?

HAUPTMANN. No, but I know I am innocent!

WILENTZ. You're the man with the will power, right?

HAUPTMANN. No.

WILENTZ. You wouldn't tell if they murdered you, would you?

HAUPTMANN. No.

WILENTZ. Will power is everything to you, isn't it?

HAUPTMANN. No, it is — I feel innocent and that gives me the power to stand up.

WILENTZ. All you have done is lie when you have sworn to God that you will tell the truth. Telling lies!

HAUPTMANN. Stop that!

WILENTZ. Didn't you swear untruths at the Bronx courthouse?

HAUPTMANN. Stop that!!

WILENTZ. Didn't you lie under oath time and time again?

HAUPTMANN. I did not!

WILENTZ. You did not?

HAUPTMANN. No!

WILENTZ. All right, sir. When they asked you if you had anymore gold certificate bills did you lie or did you tell the truth?

HAUPTMANN. I said not the truth.

WILENTZ. You lied, didn't you?

HAUPTMANN. I did, yes.

WILENTZ. Yes! Lies, lies, lies! About the Lindbergh ransom money, isn't that right?

HAUPTMANN. You lied to me too!

WILENTZ. Yes? When and where?

HAUPTMANN. Right here in this courtroom! About the wood and the writing —

WILENTZ. I see you're not smiling anymore.

HAUPTMANN. Smiling?

WILENTZ. Things have gotten a little more serious, haven't they?

HAUPTMANN. I guess this is no place for smiling.

WILENTZ. Not for you.

(WILENTZ returns to his position in the court. JUDGE TRENCHARD raps his gavel and LINDBERGH, ANNE LINDBERGH, CONDON and WILENTZ stand. They recite in unison:)

ALL. We find the defendant guilty!

(They sit. JUDGE TRENCHARD stands.)

JUDGE TRENCHARD. Bruno Richard Hauptmann. *(HAUPTMANN stands.)* You have been found guilty of the murder of Charles Lindbergh Jr. There has been no recommendation for life imprisonment. The sentence of this court is that you suffer death at a time and place and in a manner provided by law.

(He raps his gavel once more and the dumbfounded HAUPTMANN is pulled back to his cell. He sits as at the opening of the play. The guards stand around the cell and watch him. Pause.)

HAUPTMANN. It is now April 3rd, 1936. The verdict was announced on February 13th of 1935. I have been in prison awaiting execution for one year, one month and eighteen days.

I cannot express to you my feelings as I left the courtroom. I can only remember flashes — Colonel Lindbergh shaking hands with Dr. Condon; my attorney signing autographs; the judge posing for photographs; and my poor Anna ... all alone.

I will engage in no acrimony. I will not try to list the deceptions and the falsehoods used in my prosecution. I must try to live with no hatred in my heart. *(Pause.)*

They tell me that Dr. Condon is now touring the country giving lectures on how he helped to capture the Lindbergh kidnapper. He bills himself as: "Jafsie: The Man Who Convicted The Baby-Killer." He charges fifty cents for this. He is very popular, of course.

Three books have been written since the crime. Each is selling very well. Mr. Reilly is writing articles for the Hearst newspapers. And I have sold the rights to my life story to get money for my defense. That money is long since gone and my life goes on.

I wait for any news. My execution is set for tonight. Eight o' clock.

My friend Joe, who shaves me, came in and cut my hair. He told me that certain lucky people have already arrived at the prison to witness my electrocution. Thousands more line the streets outside the prison walls to wait for word that the baby-killer is dead. *(Pause.)* Where is the baby-killer? What does he think of Richard Hauptmann?

(One of the GUARDS begins to chant:)

GUARD. "Burn Hauptmann."

(Pause as HAUPTMANN listens.)

HAUPTMANN. And so they have found a chant to keep themselves warm.

(Pause as HAUPTMANN listens. The other GUARDS join the chant:)

GUARDS. "Burn   Hauptmann,   Burn   Hauptmann,   Burn Hauptmann ..."

HAUPTMANN. Little scraps of paper, little pieces of wood, and little men!

(The chant grows in intensity.)

Mein Gott! A little child has been murdered so somebody must die for it. For is not his father a great American?! And if someone does not die for the death of the child the police will be fools. So I am the one picked out to die! *(HAUPTMANN sobs. Pause.)*

(The chant slowly fades.)

Someone must die...

(ANNA steps into the light, reading a letter from HAUPTMANN.)

ANNA: "Dearest Anna,
"In an hour they will take me to the chair. I have fought with all my strength. I always thought — like a child — that the truth would save me.
"The appeals are all gone and the governor will not help. Soon I will go. Forgive me for all I may ever have done to hurt you."
HAUPTMANN. "They only want my death to end this."
ANNA. "One of my guards here told me that the Lindbergh's are planning to move away to England. It seems their new baby, Jon, has been threatened. A note got to Mrs. Lindbergh saying: 'If you like what we did to Charlie, wait until we get our hands on Jon.'"
HAUPTMANN. "Sometimes I cry for Mrs. Lindbergh too."
ANNA. "When you get this I will be dead." *(Pause.)* "Darling Anna, it really doesn't matter. They think that by killing me they will close this book. But this book, it will never close."
BOTH: "May God be with you and with our child and with all the world."

(Pause. They exchange a long look. He reaches for her. She turns and walks away, joining the impassive guards. He collapses in tears. Pause. LINDBERGH appears at the door of HAUPTMANN'S cell and enters. HAUPTMANN stands. Long pause as they stare

at each other.)

LINDBERGH. You only have about ten minutes.
HAUPTMANN. I know.
LINDBERGH. What have you been doing?
HAUPTMANN. I wrote my last words.
LINDBERGH. What were they?
HAUPTMANN. Private, to my wife. *(Pause.)* You are going to England?
LINDBERGH. It's necessary, for Anne.
HAUPTMANN. Maybe so, sad.
LINDBERGH. *(Sincerely:)* Sad. *(From the rear of the stage comes a loud whirring, grinding noise as the lights dim for a moment. LINDBERGH starts.)* What was that?
HAUPTMANN. They're testing it.
LINDBERGH. Testing ...?
HAUPTMANN. Ya.
LINDBERGH. Oh. *(Pause.)* It's not too late. You could still tell us the truth.

(HAUPTMANN smiles and sadly shakes his head. Pause.)

HAUPTMANN. I hope ... I hope your wife is better when this is over.
LINDBERGH. She hasn't slept.

(Pause.)

HAUPTMANN. *(Sincerely:)* If nothing else good comes from this I hope Mrs. Lindbergh will soon be able to sleep.

(Pause.)

LINDBERGH. Thank you. *(LINDBERGH puts out his hand. HAUPTMANN slowly shakes it.)* Look, I forgive you.
HAUPTMANN. I can't forgive. *(LINDBERGH turns to leave.)* I am innocent you know.

(LINDBERGH stops.)

LINDBERGH. So they tell me.

(LINDBERGH exits. Pause as HAUPTMANN smiles.)

HAUPTMANN *(Softly:)* Little scraps of paper, little pieces of wood, and little men.

(Two PRIESTS enter the cell. They stand on either side of HAUPTMANN and quietly recite from the Bible: Psalm 23. They read simultaneously; one in German, one in English.)

PRIEST 1. Yea, though I walk through the valley of the shadow of death, I will fear no evil: for thou art with me; thy rod and thy staff they comfort me. Thou preparest a table before me in the presence of mine enemies: thou annointest my head with oil; my cup runneth over. Surely goodness and mercy shall follow me all the days of my life: and I will dwell in the house of the Lord forever.

(Simultaneously with:)

PRIEST 2. Und ob ich schon wanderte im finstern Tal, ich furchte sein Ungluck denn du bist bei mir, dein Stechen und Stab, der trostet mich Du deckst mir den Tisch im Ungesicht meiner feinde; du salbst mein Haupt mit Oel und schenkst mir den Becher voll ein. Lauter Gluck und Gnade werden mir folgen all meine Tage, und ich werde in des Herrn Hause weilen mein Leben lang.

(As they recite and HAUPTMANN speaks, they walk slowly around the stage area — representing the walk to the execution chamber. As they walk the other guards bring their chairs to the edge of the stage and sit, like the audience, facing a single chair center stage.)

HAUPTMANN. And so this book is shut. America can now rest easily because the baby-killer is dead. America has succeeded.
The priests on either side of me are blind to it. The grey-faced

guards I pass on my last walk know a little more about it. The reporters know it. The men in business suits know it full well. The judges, the men and women know. And *he* knows it best of all. The baby-killer knows. I am as innocent as was the Lindbergh baby himself. *(Pause.)*

As he passed through the courtyard leading to the execution chamber he sees a single light in the sky. They will want some last words. *(He turns to a priest.)*

"Oh look, a star."

(Pause as the PRIESTS join the other WITNESSES watching the single chair. HAUPTMANN stands alone.)

They have given 17400 his last meal. They have slit one pant leg and one shirt sleeve to allow for the electrodes. His last walk has come. The guards move on to other men. He reaches the execution chamber like the peaceful lamb led to slaughter without a moments hesitation or revolt. He does not push or act undignified in any way. He steps into the building and through the final metal door. The final door clangs shut. It does not echo.

It is a grey room. There are lots of witnesses. He is surprised. So many. The witnesses, the lawyers, the reporters, the officers of the law, the obscene and the lucky curious all watch.

(Pause as HAUPTMANN looks at the chair. Finally he strides boldly to the chair and sits. He looks out.)

And now you can sleep. Sleep well. Sleep peacefully.

(The lights snap out.)

THE END

SKIN DEEP
Jon Lonoff

Comedy / 2m, 2f / Interior Unit Set

In *Skin Deep*, a large, lovable, lonely-heart, named Maureen Mulligan, gives romance one last shot on a blind-date with sweet awkward Joseph Spinelli; she's learned to pepper her speech with jokes to hide insecurities about her weight and appearance, while he's almost dangerously forthright, saying everything that comes to his mind. They both know they're perfect for each other, and in time they come to admit it.

They were set up on the date by Maureen's sister Sheila and her husband Squire, who are having problems of their own: Sheila undergoes a non-stop series of cosmetic surgeries to hang onto the attractive and much-desired Squire, who may or may not have long ago held designs on Maureen, who introduced him to Sheila. With Maureen particularly vulnerable to both hurting and being hurt, the time is ripe for all these unspoken issues to bubble to the surface.

"Warm-hearted comedy … the laughter was literally show-stopping. A winning play, with enough good-humored laughs and sentiment to keep you smiling from beginning to end."
– *TalkinBroadway.com*

"It's a little Paddy Chayefsky, a lot Neil Simon and a quick-witted, intelligent voyage into the not-so-tranquil seas of middle-aged love and dating. The dialogue is crackling and hilarious; the plot simple but well-turned; the characters endearing and quirky; and lurking beneath the merriment is so much heartache that you'll stand up and cheer when the unlikely couple makes it to the inevitable final clinch."
– *NYTheatreWorld.Com*

COCKEYED
William Missouri Downs

Comedy / 3m, 1f / Unit Set

Phil, an average nice guy, is madly in love with the beautiful Sophia. The only problem is that she's unaware of his existence. He tries to introduce himself but she looks right through him. When Phil discovers Sophia has a glass eye, he thinks that might be the problem, but soon realizes that she really can't see him. Perhaps he is caught in a philosophical hyperspace or dualistic reality or perhaps beautiful women are just unaware of nice guys. Armed only with a B.A. in philosophy, Phil sets out to prove his existence and win Sophia's heart. This fast moving farce is the winner of the HotCity Theatre's GreenHouse New Play Festival. The St. Louis Post-Dispatch called Cockeyed a clever romantic comedy, Talkin' Broadway called it "hilarious," while Playback Magazine said that it was "fresh and invigorating."

Winner!
of the HotCity Theatre GreenHouse New Play Festival

"Rocking with laughter...hilarious...polished and engaging work draws heavily on the age-old conventions of farce: improbable situations, exaggerated characters, amazing coincidences, absurd misunderstandings, people hiding in closets and barely missing each other as they run in and out of doors...full of comic momentum as Cockeyed hurtles toward its conclusion."
–Talkin' Broadway

TREASURE ISLAND
Ken Ludwig

All Groups / Adventure / 10m, 1f (doubling) / Areas
Based on the masterful adventure novel by Robert Louis Stevenson, *Treasure Island* is a stunning yarn of piracy on the tropical seas. It begins at an inn on the Devon coast of England in 1775 and quickly becomes an unforgettable tale of treachery and mayhem featuring a host of legendary swashbucklers including the dangerous Billy Bones (played unforgettably in the movies by Lionel Barrymore), the sinister two-timing Israel Hands, the brassy woman pirate Anne Bonney, and the hideous form of evil incarnate, Blind Pew. At the center of it all are Jim Hawkins, a 14-year-old boy who longs for adventure, and the infamous Long John Silver, who is a complex study of good and evil, perhaps the most famous hero-villain of all time. Silver is an unscrupulous buccaneer-rogue whose greedy quest for gold, coupled with his affection for Jim, cannot help but win the heart of every soul who has ever longed for romance, treasure and adventure.

THE OFFICE PLAYS
Two full length plays by Adam Bock

THE RECEPTIONIST
Comedy / 2m, 2f / Interior

At the start of a typical day in the Northeast Office, Beverly deals effortlessly with ringing phones and her colleague's romantic troubles. But the appearance of a charming rep from the Central Office disrupts the friendly routine. And as the true nature of the company's business becomes apparent, The Receptionist raises disquieting, provocative questions about the consequences of complicity with evil.

"...Mr. Bock's poisoned Post-it note of a play."
– *New York Times*

"Bock's intense initial focus on the routine goes to the heart of *The Receptionist's* pointed, painfully timely allegory... elliptical, provocative play..."
– *Time Out New York*

THE THUGS
Comedy / 2m, 6f / Interior

The Obie Award winning dark comedy about work, thunder and the mysterious things that are happening on the 9th floor of a big law firm. When a group of temps try to discover the secrets that lurk in the hidden crevices of their workplace, they realize they would rather believe in gossip and rumors than face dangerous realities.

"Bock starts you off giggling, but leaves you with a chill."
– *Time Out New York*

"... a delightfully paranoid little nightmare that is both more chillingly realistic and pointedly absurd than anything John Grisham ever dreamed up."
– *New York Times*

SAMUELFRENCH.COM

NO SEX PLEASE, WE'RE BRITISH
Anthony Marriott and Alistair Foot

Farce / 7 m, 3 f / Interior

A young bride who lives above a bank with her husband who is the assistant manager, innocently sends a mail order off for some Scandinavian glassware. What comes is Scandinavian pornography. The plot revolves around what is to be done with the veritable floods of pornography, photographs, books, films and eventually girls that threaten to engulf this happy couple. The matter is considerably complicated by the man's mother, his boss, a visiting bank inspector, a police superintendent and a muddled friend who does everything wrong in his reluctant efforts to set everything right, all of which works up to a hilarious ending of closed or slamming doors. This farce ran in London over eight years and also delighted Broadway audiences.

"Titillating and topical."
– NBC TV

"A really funny Broadway show."
– ABC TV

ANON
Kate Robin

Drama / 2m, 12f / Area

Anon. follows two couples as they cope with sexual addiction. Trip and Allison are young and healthy, but he's more interested in his abnormally large porn collection than in her. While they begin to work through both of their own sexual and relationship hang-ups, Trip's parents are stuck in the roles they've been carving out for years in their dysfunctional marriage. In between scenes with these four characters, 10 different women, members of a support group for those involved with individuals with sex addiction issues, tell their stories in monologues that are alternately funny and harrowing..

In addition to Anon., Robin's play What They Have was also commissioned by South Coast Repertory. Her plays have also been developed at Manhattan Theater Club, Playwrights Horizons, New York Theatre Workshop, The Eugene O'Neill Theater Center's National Playwrights Conference, JAW/West at Portland Center Stage and Ensemble Studio Theatre. Television and film credits include "Six Feet Under" (writer/supervising producer) and "Coming Soon." Robin received the 2003 Princess Grace Statuette for playwriting and is an alumna of New Dramatists.

WHITE BUFFALO
Don Zolidis

Drama / 3m, 2f (plus chorus)/ Unit Set

Based on actual events, WHITE BUFFALO tells the story of the miracle birth of a white buffalo calf on a small farm in southern Wisconsin. When Carol Gelling discovers that one of the buffalo on her farm is born white in color, she thinks nothing more of it than a curiosity. Soon, however, she learns that this is the fulfillment of an ancient prophecy believed by the Sioux to bring peace on earth and unity to all mankind. Her little farm is quickly overwhelmed with religious pilgrims, bringing her into contact with a culture and faith that is wholly unfamiliar to her. When a mysterious businessman offers to buy the calf for two million dollars, Carol is thrown into doubt about whether to profit from the religious beliefs of others or to keep true to a spirituality she knows nothing about.